City of Truth

CITY OF TRUTH

James Morrow

Illustrated by Steve Crisp

St. Martin's Press
New York

CITY OF TRUTH. Copyright © 1990 by James Morrow. All rights reserved.
Printed in the United States of America. No part of this book may be used or
reproduced in any manner whatsoever without written permission except in the
case of brief quotations embodied in critical articles or reviews. For information,
address St. Martin's Press, 175 Fifth Avenue, New York, N.Y. 10010.

Library of Congress Cataloging-in-Publication Data

Morrow, James.
    City of truth / James Morrow.
       p.   cm.
    ISBN 0-312-07672-X
    I. Title.
    PS3563.0876C57   1992
    813'.54—dc20   92-2981
                                         CIP

First published in Great Britain by Random Century Group.

First U.S. Edition: June 1992
10 9 8 7 6 5 4 3 2 1

I am grateful to Linda Barnes, Margaret Duda, Jean Morrow, John O'Connor, Kathy Smith, James Stevens-Arce and Michael Svoboda for their candid comments on the manuscript.

To my mother
EMILY MORROW
for her love
and integrity

1

I no longer live in the City of Truth. I have exiled myself from Veritas, from all cities – from the world. The room in which I'm writing is cramped as a county jail and moist as a lung, but I'm learning to call it home. My only light is a candle, a fat, butter-coloured stalk from which nets of melted wax hang like cobwebs. I wonder what it would be like to live in that candle – in the translucent crannies that surround the flame: a fine abode, warm, safe and snug. I imagine myself spending each day wandering waxen passageways and sitting in paraffin parlours, each night lying in bed listening to the steady drip-drip-drip of my home consuming itself.

My name is Jack Sperry, and I am thirty-eight years old. I was born in truth's own city, Veritas, on the last day of its bicentennial year. Like many boys of my generation, I dreamed of becoming an art critic one day: the pure primal thrill of attacking a painting, the sheer visceral kick of savaging a movie or a poem. In my case, however, the dream turned into reality, for by my twenty-second year I was employed as a deconstructionist down at the Wittgenstein Museum in Plato Borough, giving illusion its due.

Other dreams – wife, children, happy home – came harder. From the very first Helen and I wrestled with the thorny Veritasian question of whether *love* was a truthful term for how we felt about each other – such a misused notion, *love*, a kind of one-word lie – a problem we began ignoring once a more concrete crisis had taken its place.

His sperm are lazy, she thought. Her eggs are duds, I decided. But at last we found the right doctor, the proper pill, and suddenly there was Toby, flourishing inside Helen's redeemed womb: Toby the embryo; Toby the baby; Toby the toddler; Toby the preschool carpenter, forever churning out crooked birdhouses, lopsided napkin holders, and asymmetrical bookends; Toby the boy naturalist, befriending every slithery, slimy, misbegotten creature ever to wriggle across the face of the Earth. This was a child with a maggot farm. A roach ranch. A pet slug. 'I think I love him,' I told Helen one day. 'Let's not get carried away,' she replied.

The morning I met Martina Coventry, Toby was off at Camp Ditch-the-Kids in the untamed outskirts of Kant Borough. He sent us a picture postcard every day, a routine that, I realize in retrospect, was a kind of smuggling operation; once Toby got home, the postcards would all be *there*, waiting to join his vast collection.

To wit:

Dear Mom and Dad: Today we learned how to survive in case we're ever lost in the woods – what kind of bark to eat and stuff. Counsellor Rick says he never heard of anybody actually using these skills. Your son, *Toby*.

And also:

Dear Mom and Dad: There's a big rat trap in the pantry here, and guess who always sneaks in at night and finds out what animal got caught and then sets it free? Me! Counsellor Rick says we're boring. Your son, *Toby*.

It was early, barely 7 a.m., but already Booze Before Breakfast was jammed to its crumbling brick walls. I made my way through a conglomeration of cigarette smoke and beer fumes, through frank sweat and honest halitosis. A jukebox thumped out Probity singing 'Copingly Ever After'. The saloon keeper, Jimmy Breeze, brought me the usual – a raspberry Danish and a Bloody Mary – setting them on the splintery cedar bar. I told him I had no cash but would pay him tomorrow. This was Veritas. I would.

I spotted only one free chair – at a tiny, circular table across from a young woman whose wide face and plump contours boasted, to this beholder's eye, the premier sensuality of a Rubens model. Peter Paul Rubens was much on my mind just then, for I'd recently criticized not only *The Garden of Love* but also *The Raising of the Cross*.

'Come here often?' she asked as I approached, my plastic-wrapped Danish poised precariously atop my drink. Her abundant terra-cotta hair was compacted into a modest bun. Her ankle-length green dress was made of guileless cambric.

I sat down. 'Uh-huh,' I mumbled, pushing aside the sugar bowl, the napkin dispenser and the woman's orange peels to make room for my Bloody and Danish. 'I always stop in on my way to the Wittgenstein.'

'You a critic?' Even in the endemic gloom of Booze Before Breakfast, her smooth, unpainted skin glowed.

I nodded. 'Jack Sperry.'

'Can't say I'm impressed. It doesn't take much intellectual prowess, does it?'

She could be as honest as she liked, provided I could watch her voluptuous lips move. 'What line are *you* in?' I asked.

'I'm a writer.' Her eyes expanded: limpid, generous eyes, the cobalt blue of Salome's So-So Contraceptive Cream. 'It has its dangers, of course. There's always that risk of falling into . . . what's it called?'

'Metaphor?'

'Metaphor.'

There were no metaphors in Veritas. Metaphors were lies. Flesh could be *like* grass, but it never *was* grass. Use a metaphor in Veritas, and your conditioning instantly possessed you, hammering your skull, searing your heart, dropping you straight to hell in a bucket of pain. So to speak.

'What do you write?' I asked.

'Doggerel. Greeting-card messages, advertising jingles, inspirational verses like you see in—'

'Sell much?'

A grimace distorted her luminous face. 'I should say I'm an *aspiring* writer.'

'I'd like to read some of your doggerel,' I asserted. 'And I'd like to have sex with you,' I added, wincing at my candour. It wasn't easy being a citizen.

Her grimace intensified.

'Sorry if I'm being offensive,' I said. 'Am I being offensive?'

3

'You're being offensive.'

'Offensive only in the abstract, or offensive to you personally?'

'Both.' She slid a wedge of orange into her wondrous mouth. 'Are you married?'

'Yes.'

'A good marriage?'

'Pretty good.' *To have and to hold, to love and to cherish, to the degree that these mischievous and sentimental abstractions possess any meaning*: Helen and I had opted for a traditional ceremony. 'Our son is terrific. I think I love him.'

'If we had an affair' – a furtive smile – 'wouldn't you feel guilty?'

'I've never cheated.' An affair, I mused. Scary stuff. 'Guilt? Yes, of course.' I sipped my Bloody Mary. 'I believe I could tolerate it.'

'Well, you can drop the whole fantasy, Mr Sperry,' the young woman said, a declaration that filled me with an odd mixture of relief and disappointment. 'You can put the entire thought out of your—'

'Call me Jack.' I unpackaged my Danish; the wrapper dragged away clots of vanilla icing like a Band-Aid pulling off a scab. 'And you're . . . ?'

'Martina Coventry, and at the moment I feel only a mild, easily controlled desire to copulate with you.'

' "At the moment",' I repeated, marvelling at how much ambiguity could be wedged into a prepositional phrase. In a fashionably gauche move I licked the icing off the Danish wrapper (*The Mendacity of Manners* had recently hit the top slot on the *Times* best-seller list). 'Will you show me your doggerel?' I asked.

'It's bad doggerel.'

'Doggerel is by definition bad.'

'Mine's worse.'

'Please.'

Martina's pliant features contracted into a bemused frown. 'There's a great deal of sexual tension occurring between us now, wouldn't you say?'

'Correct.'

She reached into her purse and pulled out a folded sheet

of crisp white typing paper, pressing it into my palm with a sheepish wink.

First came a Valentine's Day message.

> I find you somewhat interesting,
> You're not too short or tall,
> And if you'd be my Valentine,
> I wouldn't mind at all.

A birthday greeting followed.

> Roses drop dead,
> Violets do too,
> With each day life gets shorter,
> Happy birthday to you.

'I have no illusions about earning a living from my doggerel,' said Martina, understating the case radically. 'What I'd really like is a career writing political speeches. My borough rep almost hired me to run his re-election campaign. "Cold in person, but highly efficient" – that was the slogan I worked out. In the end, his girlfriend got the job. Do you like my verses, Jack?'

'They're awful.'

'I'm going to burn them.' Martina kissed an orange slice, sucked out the juice.

'No. Don't. I'd like to have them.'

'You would? Why?'

'Because I'm anticipating you'll write something else on the page.' From my shirt pocket I produced a ballpoint pen (*Paradox Pen Company – Random Leaks Common*). 'Like, say, the information I'll need to find you again.'

'So we can have an affair?'

'The thought terrifies me.'

'You *are* fairly attractive,' Martina observed, taking the pen. Indeed. It's the eyebrows that do it, great bushy extrusions suggesting a predatory mammal of unusual prowess – wolf, bear, leopard – though they draw plenty of support from my straight nose and square jaw. Only when you get to my chin, a pointy, pimply knoll forever covered with stubble, does the illusion of perfection dissolve. 'I'm

5

warning you, Jack, I have my own Smith and Wesson Liberalstopper.' She signed her name in bold curlicues across the bottom of the page, added her address and phone number. 'Try to force yourself on me and I'll shoot to kill.'

I lifted the doggerel from the table, flicking a Danish crumb from the word *Valentine*. 'Funny – you've *almost* told a lie here. Roses don't drop dead, they—'

'They wither.'

'If I were you, Martina, I wouldn't take such chances with my sanity.'

'If you were me,' she replied, 'you *would* take such chances with your sanity, because otherwise you'd be someone else.'

'True enough,' I said, pocketing Martina Coventry's stultifying verses.

Galileo Square was clogged with traffic, a dense metallic knot betokening a delay of at least twenty minutes. I flipped on my Plymouth Adequate's radio, tuned in WTRU, and began waiting it out. Eighteenth Street, Nineteenth Street, Twentieth . . .

' . . . fact that I accepted a fifty-thousand-dollar kickback during the Avelthorpe Tariff Scandal should not, I feel, detract from my record on education, the environment, and medical . . .'

Twenty-fifth Street, Twenty-sixth Street, Twenty-seventh . . .

' . . . for while we do indeed divert an enormous amount of protein that might help relieve world hunger, the psychological benefits of dogs and cats have been proved almost beyond the shadow of a . . .'

Thirtieth Street, Thirty-first . . .

' . . . displeased with the unconscionable quantities of sugar we were putting in children's cereals, and so we're happy to announce a new policy of . . .'

At last: the Wittgenstein Museum, a one-storey brick building sprawling across a large concrete courtyard, flanked by a Brutality Squad station on the north side and a café called the Dirty Dog on the south. The guard, a toothy, clean-cut young man with a Remington Metapenis

6

strapped to his waist, waved me through the iron gates. I headed for the parking lot. Derrick Popkes of the Egyptian Relics Division had beaten me to my usual space, usurping it with his Ford Sufficient, so I had to drive all the way to the main incinerator and park by the coal bin.

'Channel your violent impulses in a salutary direction – become a Marine. Purge your natural tendency toward—' I silenced the radio, killed the engine.

What had life been like during the Age of Lies? How had the human mind endured a world where politicians misled, advertisers overstated, clerics exaggerated, women wore make-up, and people professed love at the drop of a tropological hat? How had humanity survived the epoch we'd all read about in the history books, those nightmare centuries of casuistic customs and fraudulent rites? The idea confounded me. It rattled me to the core. The Easter Bunny, the Tooth Fairy, Santa Claus, Frosty the Snowman, Rudolph the Red-Nosed Reindeer: staggering.

'You're late,' observed the chief curator, bald and portly Arnold Cook, as I strolled into the front office. 'Heavy traffic?'

'Yes.' I slid my card into the time clock, felt the jolt of its mechanism imprinting my tardiness. 'Bumper to bumper.' Every so often, you'd experience an urge to stop short of total candour. But then suddenly it would come: a dull neurological throb that, if you didn't tell the whole truth, would quickly bloom into a psychosomatic explosion in your skull. 'I also wasted a lot of time getting a young woman's address.'

'Do you expect to copulate with her?' Mr Cook asked, following me to the changing room. Early morning, yet already he was coated with characteristic sweat, droplets that, as I once told him in a particularly painful exercise of civic duty, put me in mind of my cat's litter box.

Denim overalls drooped from the lockers. I selected a pair that looked about my size. 'Adultery is deceitful,' I reminded the curator.

'So is fidelity,' he replied. 'In its own way.'

'In its own way,' I agreed, donning my overalls.

I followed a nonliteral rat-maze of dark, dusty corridors

to my workshop. It was packed. As usual, the items I was supposed to analyse that day divided equally into the authentic *objets d'artifice* unearthed by the archaeologists and the ersatz output of the city's furtive malcontents – its 'dissemblers'. For every statue from ancient Greece, there was a clumsy forgery. For every Cézanne, a feeble imitation. For every eighteenth-century novel, the effluvium of a vanity press.

The dissemblers. Even now, after all I've been through, the word sends a cold wind through my bones. The dissemblers: Veritas's own enemy within, defacing its walls with their oil paintings, befouling its air with their songs and, most daringly, turning its pristine streets into forums for Sophocles, Shakespeare, Ibsen and Shaw, each production a ragged, jerry-built affair frantically staged before the Brutality Squad could arrive and chase the outlaw actors into their holes and hide-outs. Only once had a dissembler been caught, and then the Squad had bungled it, clubbing the woman to death before they could ask the crucial question.

How do you tell lies without going mad?
How?

What I loved about this job was the way it got my head and my hands working together. True, the raw existential act of deconstruction was rather crude, but before that moment you had to use your mind; you had to decide that the piece in question, whether original or forgery, was indeed inimical to the public good.

I turned toward a piece of classical mendacity labelled *Nike of Samothrace*. A lie? Yes, manifestly: those wings. Merely to behold such a creature nauseated me. No wonder Plato had banned artists and playwrights from his hypothetical utopia. 'Three removes from nature,' he'd called them, three removes from factuality. ART IS A LIE, the electric posters in Circumspect Park reminded us. Truth might be beauty, but it simply didn't work the other way around.

Like an agoraphobic preparing for an indoor picnic, I spread my canvas dropcloth on the concrete floor. I took down a No. 7 sledge hammer. The *Nike* had arrived

8

headless, and now, as I wielded my critical apparatus against her, she became wingless as well – now breastless, now hipless. Amorphous chunks of marble littered the dropcloth. My overalls stank of sweat, my tongue felt like a dried fig wedged into my mouth. An exhausting enterprise, criticism; gruelling work, analysis. I deserved a break.

A note lay on the desk in my coffee cubicle. 'Dear Mr Sperry: Last Friday, you might recall, you offered to write a letter on my behalf,' I read as the water boiled. 'I hope Mr Cook might receive it by the end of the week. Fairly sincere regards, *Stanley Marcus*.'

I took down my mug, dumped in a heaping teaspoonful of semi-instant crystals – Donaldson's Drinkable Coffee, my favourite brand – added hot water from my kettle, and began mentally composing a recommendation for Stanley. He'd been assisting in my sector for over a year now, servicing a dozen of us critics – sharpening our axes, fuelling our blowtorches, faithfully sweeping up our workshops and cubicles – and now he was looking to get promoted. 'In all honesty, I believe Stanley would prove reasonably competent at running the main incinerator. Of course, he is something of a drudge and a toady, but those qualities may actually serve him well. One thing you'll notice about Stanley is that he farts a great deal, but here again we're not talking about a characteristic that would hinder . . .'

I glanced at my *Beatoff Magazine* calendar – and a good thing, or I might have forgotten about meeting my wife for lunch. 'Helen,' said the 9 July square, '1 p.m., No Great Shakes.' No Great Shakes on Twenty-ninth Street had marvellous submarine sandwiches and terrific Waldorf salads. Its shakes were not so great.

Miss July – Wendy Warren, according to the accompanying profile – leered at me from the glossy paper. 'Being an intellectual,' ran her capsule biography, 'Wendy proved most articulate on the subject of posing for us. "It's at once tawdry and exhilarating, humiliating and energizing," she said. "If not for the quick five thousand, I never would've considered it." When we learned how smart she was – that Interborough Chess Championship and everything – we almost disqualified her. However, we knew that many of you would enjoy masturbating to . . .'

Good old Wendy. My hypothetical id was ticking. And suddenly I realized there'd be a minor but irrefutable thrill in simply looking at Martina Coventry's handwriting, as if its twists and turns were the lines of her Rubensian flesh. I took a long sip of Donaldson's Drinkable and, pulling Martina's doggerel from my pocket, flattened the crumpled sheet on the desk.

The verses were as terrible as ever, but the signature indeed held a certain eroticism. I even got a mild charge from the contours of the subsequent information. '7 Lacklustre Lane, Descartes Borough,' she'd written. 'Phone 610–400.'

Something caught my eye, a web of thin shallow grooves in the paper, occupying in the space between the Valentine message and the birthday greeting, and I realized that the object in my possession had backstopped one of Martina's earlier creative convulsions. Curious, I seized the nearest pencil and began rubbing graphite across the page, causing the older verses to materialize like a photographic image appearing in a tray of developer. Within seconds the entire composition lay before me, and my nervous system vibrated with intermingled disbelief, horror and fascination.

Lies.

Gruesome and poetic lies.

In Martina Coventry's own hand.

> I hide my wings inside my soul,
> Their feathers soft and dry,
> And when the world's not looking,
> I take them out and fly.

Sweat erupted in my palms and along my brow. *Wings*. Martina didn't have wings. No one did. Who did she think she was, the Nike of Samothrace? One might as well assert the reality of Santa Claus or Lewis Carroll's Alice. As for the *soul*, that soggy construct . . .

Perhaps my eyes were deceiving me. I resolved to read the poem aloud – hearing is believing; to sense these astonishing words resounding in my head would be to know they in fact existed. 'I hide my wings,' I said in a hoarse whisper, but I couldn't go on. A primordial terror surged up, bringing a migraine so severe I almost fainted.

My critical instincts took hold. I seized Martina's poem, dashed out of the museum and ran across the courtyard to the main incinerator. Skull throbbing, I thrust the page toward the same seething pit where the day before I had deconstructed a dozen books on reincarnation and the last two hundred issues of *The Journal of Psychic Healing*.

I stopped.

Was I in fact ready to cast Martina Coventry out of my life? Was I truly willing to consign her identity to the flames? No. I wasn't. I fixed on her address, massaging it into my memory.

How did she tell lies without going mad?

How?

Phone 610–400. No problem. For his *sixth* birthday we'd given Toby a *ten*-speed bike, but *four* months went by before I put it together, and he hardly ever rode it, so the whole experience was rather null, a zero – two, in fact. 6 . . . 1 . . . 0 . . . 4 . . . 0 . . . 0.

My fingers parted, and the poems floated toward their fate, joining the Homer epics, the Racine plays, the Dickens novels and the mushy, gushy, pseudoscientific rantings of *The Journal of Psychic Healing*.

'It's absolutely incredible,' I told Helen as we sat in No Great Shakes burrowing into the day's special: MURDERED COW SANDWICH, WILTED HEARTS OF LETTUCE, HIGH-CHOLESTEROL FRIES – A QUITE REASONABLE $5.99. 'Four hours ago I was having breakfast with a dissembler. I could've reached out and touched her.'

'But you didn't,' said Helen in a tone more apprehensive than assured. She slid her sunglasses upward into her frothy, greying hair, the better to scrutinize my face.

'I didn't.'

'She's definitely one of them?'

'I'm positive. More or less.'

11

My wife looked straight at me, a shred of lettuce drooping over her lips like a green tongue. 'Let's not get carried away,' she said.

Let's not get carried away. That was Helen's motto; it belonged on her tombstone. She was a woman who'd devoted her life to not getting carried away – in her career, in our bed, anywhere. It was her job, I believe, that made her so sedate. As a stringer for the celebrated supermarket tabloid, *Sweet Reason*, Helen moved among the sceptics and logicians of the world, collecting scoops: CONTROLLED STUDY NEGATES NEW ARTHRITIS CURE, SLAIN BIGFOOT REVEALED AS SCHIZOPHRENIC IN SUIT, TOP PSYCHICS' PREDICTIONS FALL FLAT. Ten years of writing such stories, and you acquire a bit of a chill.

I said, 'You have a better interpretation, ostensible darling?'

'Maybe she found the paper on the street, supposed sweetheart,' Helen replied. A beautiful woman, I'd always thought: large pleading eyes, soft round cheeks you wanted to rub against your hands like balm. 'Maybe somebody *else* composed the poem.'

'It was in Martina's handwriting.'

Helen bit into her murdered cow. 'Let me guess. She gave you her name and address, right?'

'Yes. She wrote them on the page.'

'Did she say she wanted to have sex with you?'

'Not in so many words.'

'Did you say you wanted to have sex with her?'

'Yes.'

'You think you will?'

'I don't know,' I said. 'I hope so, I hope not – you know how it is.' I licked the grease from a French fry. 'I'd hate to hurt you,' I added.

Helen's eyes became as dark and narrow as slots in a gun turret. 'I probably feel as conflicted as you. Part of me wants you to turn this Martina over to the Brutality Squad, the better to get her out of our lives forever. The other part, the woman who feels a certain undeniable affection for you, knows that would be a stupid thing to do, because

12

if the lady senses the police are on her trail, well, she might also sense how they got there, right? These dissemblers, I've heard, are no nonliteral pussycats. They've got assassins in their ranks.'

'Assassins,' I concurred. 'Assassins, terrorists, lunatics. You want me to burn the paper?'

'Burn it, critic.'

'I did.'

My wife smiled. In Veritas, one never asked, *Really? Are you kidding? Do you mean that?* She finished her cow and said, 'You're a somewhat better man than I thought.'

We filled the rest of the hour with the usual marital battles – such ironically allied words, *marital, martial*. Helen and I loved to fight. My erections were becoming increasingly less substantive, she asserted, truthfully. The noises she made when chewing her food were disgusting, I reported, honestly. She told me she had no intention of procuring the obligatory gift for my niece's brainburn party on Saturday – Connie wasn't *her* niece. I didn't *want* her to get the gift, I retorted, because she'd buy something cheap, obvious and otherwise emblematic of the contempt in which she held my sister. And so we continued, straight through coffee and dessert, nibbling at each other like mice, picking each other off like snipers. Such fun, such pathological fun.

Helen reached into her handbag and pulled out a crisp sheet of computer paper speckled with dot-matrix characters. 'This came this morning,' she explained. 'A rabbit bit Toby,' she announced evenly.

'A what? Rabbit? What are you talking about?'

'He's probably forgotten the whole thing by now.'

'It *bit* him?'

Ralph Kitto
Executive Director
Camp Ditch-the-Kids
Box 145
Kant Borough

Mr and Mrs Sperry:

As you may know, your son makes it his annoying mission to

release all the animals caught in our rat trap. Yesterday, in performing one such act of ambiguous compassion, he was attacked by a rare species called Hob's hare. We dressed his wound immediately and, checking his medical records, confirmed that his tetanus immunizations are up to date.

As a safety precaution, we retained the rabbit and placed it under quarantine. I am moderately sorry to report that today the animal died. We forthwith froze the corpse then shipped it to the Kraft Epidemiological Institute. The Kraft doctors will contact you if there's anything to worry about, though I suspect you've started worrying already.

Yours up to a point,
Ralph Kitto

'Why didn't you show me this right away?'

Helen shrugged. 'It's not a big deal.'

Smooth, nervy Helen. There were times when I wondered whether she liked Toby. 'Aren't you bothered that the rabbit died?'

'Maybe it was old.'

My teeth came together in a tight, dense grid. The thought of Toby's pain troubled me. Not his physical pain – it might have even done him some good, toughening him up for his brainburn. What distressed me was the sense of betrayal he must have felt; my son had always negotiated with the world in good faith, and now the world had bitten him. 'There's something I should tell you,' I admitted to my wife. 'Before burning Martina's doggerel, I memorized her address and phone number.'

Helen appeared to be experiencing a bad odour. 'How readily you exhibit the same disgusting qualities one associates with anuses. Honestly, Jack, sometimes I wonder why we got married.'

'Sometimes I wonder the same thing. I wish that rabbit hadn't died.'

'Forget the rabbit. We're talking about why I married you.'

'You married me,' I said, telling the truth, 'because you thought I was your last chance.'

14

2

Saturday: pigs have wings, dogs can talk, money grows on trees – like some mindless and insistent song the litany wove through me, rolling amid the folds of my cerebrum as it always did when one of my nieces was scheduled to get burned. Stones are alive, rats chase cats – ten lies all told, a decalogue of deceit, resting at our city's core like a dragon sleeping beside a subterranean treasure. Salt is sweet, the Pope is Jewish – and suddenly the child has done it, suddenly she's thrown off the corrupt mantle of youth and put on the innocence of adulthood. Suddenly she's a woman.

I awoke aggressively that morning, tearing the blankets away as if nothing else stood between myself and total alertness. Across the room, my wife slept peacefully, indifferent to the world's sad truths, its dead rabbits. Ours was a two-bed marriage. The symbolism was not lost on me. Often we made love on the floor – in the narrow, neutral territory between our mattresses, our conjugal Geneva.

Yawning, I charged into the shower stall, where warm water poured forth the instant the sensors detected me. The TV receiver winked on – the *Enduring Another Day* programme. Grimacing under the studio lights, our Assistant Secretary of Imperialism discussed the city's growing involvement in the Hegelian Civil War. 'So far, over four thousand Veritasian combat troops have died,' the interviewer noted as I lathered up with Bourgeois Soap. 'A senseless loss,' the secretary replied cheerfully. 'Our policy is impossible to justify on rational grounds, which is why we've started invoking national security and other shibboleths.'

I left the shower and padded bare-assed into the bedroom. Clothes *per se* were deceitful, of course, but nudity carried its own measure of compromise, a continual tacit message of provocation and come-hither. I dressed. Nothing disingenuous: underwear, a collarless shirt, a grey Age-of-Lies suit with the lapels cut off. Our apartment was similarly sparse, peeled to a core of rectitude. Many of our friends had curtains, wall hangings and rugs, but not Helen and I. We were patriotic.

The odour of stale urine hit me as I approached the elevator. How unfortunate that some people translated the ban on sexually segregated rest rooms – PRIVACY IS A LIE, the huge flashing billboard on Voltaire Avenue reminded us – into a general fear of toilets. Hadn't they heard of public health? Public health was guileless.

I descended, crossed the lobby, encapsulated myself in the revolving door, and exited into Veritas's thick and gritty air. Sprinkled with soot, my Adequate lay on the far side of Eighty-second Street. In the old days, I'd heard, you never knew for sure that your car would be unmolested, or even there, when you left it overnight. Dishonesty was so rampant, you started your engine with a key.

I zoomed past the imperially functional cinderblocks that constituted City Hall, reaching the market district shortly before noon. Bless my luck, a parking spot lay directly in front of Molly's Rather Expensive Toy Store – such joy in emptiness, I mused, such satisfaction in a void.

'My, aren't *you* a pretty fellow?' a hawk-faced female clerk sang out as I strode through Molly's door. Pricey marionettes dangled from the ceiling like victims of a mass lynching. 'Except, of course, for that chin.'

'Your body's arousing enough,' I replied, casting a candid eye up and down the clerk. A Bertrand Russell University T-shirt moulded itself around her breasts. Grimy white slacks encased her thighs. 'But that nose,' I added forlornly. A demanding business, citizenship.

She tapped my wedding ring and glowered. 'What brings you here? Something for your mistress's kid sister?'

'My niece is getting burned today.'

'And you're waiting till the last minute to buy her a present?'

'True.'

'Roller skates are popular. We sold fifteen pairs last month. Three were returned as defective.'

'Lead the way.'

I followed her past racks of baseball gloves and stuffed animals and up to a bin filled with roller skates, the new six-wheeler style with miniature jets in the heels. 'The laces break in ten per cent of cases,' the clerk confessed. 'Last April an engine exploded – maybe you saw the story on TV – and the poor girl, you know what happened? She got pitched into a culvert and cracked her skull and died.'

'I believe Connie likes yellow,' I said, taking down a pair of skates the colour of Mom's Middling Margarine. 'One size fits all?'

'More or less.'

'Your price as good as anybody's else's?'

'You can get the same thing for two dollars less at Marquand's.'

'Haven't the time. Can you gift-wrap them?'

'Not skilfully.'

'Sold.'

I'd promised Gloria I wouldn't just go to Connie's post-treatment party – I would attend the burn as well, doing what I could to keep the kid's morale up. Normally both parents were present, but that deplorable person Peter Raymond couldn't be bothered. 'I've seen better parenting at the zoo,' Helen liked to say of my ex-brother-in-law. 'I know wart hogs who are better fathers.'

You could find a burn hospital in practically every neighbourhood, but Gloria had insisted on the best, Veteran's Shock Institute in Spinoza Borough, a smoke-stained pile of bricks overlooking the Giordano Bruno Bridge. Entering, I noticed a crowd of ten-year-olds jamming the central holding area; it seemed more like the platform of a train station than the waiting room of a hospital, the girls hanging together in nervous, chattering clusters, trying to comfort each other, the boys engaged in mock gunfights around the potted palms, distracting themselves with pseudo violence, pretending not to be terrified of what the day would bring.

Tucking the indifferently wrapped skates under my arm, I ascended to the second floor. WARNING: THIS ELEVATOR MAINTAINED BY PEOPLE WHO HATE THEIR JOBS. RIDE AT YOUR OWN RISK.

My niece was already in her glass cell, dressed in a green smock and bound to the chair via leather thongs, one electrode strapped to her left arm, another to her right leg. Black wires trailed from the copper terminals like threads spun by some vile and poisonous spider Toby would have adopted. She welcomed me with a brave smile, and I pointed to her gift, hoping to raise her spirits, however briefly.

Clipboard in hand, a short, cherubic doctor with MERRICK affixed to his tunic entered the cell and snugged a copper helmet over my niece's cranium. I gave her a thumbs-up signal. Soon it will be over, kid – snow is hot, grass is purple, all of it.

'Thanks for coming,' said Gloria, taking my arm and guiding me into the observation booth. 'How's the family?'

'A rabbit attacked Toby.'

'A *rabbit*?'

'And then it died.'

'I'm glad somebody besides me has problems,' she admitted.

My sister was a rather attractive woman – glossy black hair, pristine skin, a better chin than mine – but today she looked terrible: the anticipation, the fear. I was actually present when her marriage collapsed. The three of us were sitting in Booze Before Breakfast, and suddenly she said to Peter, 'I sometimes worry that you copulate with Ellen Lambert – do you?'

And Peter said yes, he did. And Gloria said you fucker. And Peter said right. And Gloria asked how many others. And Peter said lots. And Gloria asked why – did he do it to strengthen the marriage? And Peter said no, he just liked to ejaculate inside other women.

After patting Connie on her rust-coloured bangs, Merrick joined us in the booth. 'Morning, folks,' he said, his cheer a precarious mix of the genuine and the forced. 'How're we doing here?'

18

'Do you care?' my sister asked.

'Hard to say.' The doctor fanned me with his clipboard. 'Your husband?'

'Brother,' Gloria explained.

'Jack Sperry,' I said.

'Glad you could make it, Sperry,' said the doctor. 'When there's only one family member out here, the kid'll sometimes go catatonic on us.' Merrick shoved the clipboard toward Gloria. 'Informed consent, right?'

'They told me the possibilities.' She studied the clipboard. 'Cardiac—'

'Cardiac arrest, cerebral haemorrhage, respiratory failure, kidney damage,' Merrick recited.

Gloria scrawled her signature. 'When was the last time anything like that happened?'

'They killed a little boy over at Veritas Memorial on Tuesday,' said Merrick, edging toward the control panel. 'A freak thing, but now and then we really screw up. Everybody ready?'

'Not really,' said my sister.

Merrick pushed a button, and PIGS HAVE WINGS materialized before my niece on a lucite tachistoscope screen. Seeing the falsehood, the doctor, Gloria, and I shuddered in unison.

'Can you hear me, lassie?' Merrick inquired into the microphone.

Connie opened her mouth, and a feeble 'Yes' dribbled out of the loudspeaker.

'You see those words?' Merrick asked. The lurid red characters hovered in the air like weary butterflies.

'Y-yes.'

'When I give the order, read them aloud.'

'Is it going to hurt?' my niece quavered.

'It's going to hurt a lot. Will you read the words when I say so?'

'I'm scared. Do I have to?'

'You have to.' Merrick rested a pudgy finger on the switch. 'Now!'

' "P-pigs have wings." '

And so it began, this bris of the human conscience,

19

this electroconvulsive rite of passage. Merrick nudged the switch. The volts ripped through Connie. She let out a sharp scream and turned the colour of stucco.

'But they don't,' she gasped. 'Pigs don't . . .'

My own burn flooded back. The outrage, the agony.

'You're right, lass – they don't.' Merrick gave the voltage regulator a subtle twist, and Gloria flinched. 'You did reasonably well, girl,' the doctor continued, handing the mike to my sister.

'Oh, yes, Connie,' she said. 'Keep up the awfully good work.'

'It's not fair.' Sweat speckled Connie's forehead. 'I want to go home.'

As Gloria surrendered the mike, the tachistoscope projected SNOW IS HOT. My brain reeled with the lie.

'Now, lass! Read it!'

' "S-s-snow is . . . h-hot." ' Lightning struck. Connie howled. Blood rolled over her lower lip. During my own burn, I'd practically bitten my tongue off. 'I don't want this any more,' she wailed.

'It's not a choice, lass.'

'Snow is *cold*.' Tears threaded Connie's freckles together. 'Please stop hurting me.'

'Cold. Right. Smart girl.' Merrick cranked up the voltage. 'Ready, Connie? Here it comes.'

HORSES HAVE SIX LEGS.

'Why do I have to do this? *Why?*'

'Everybody does it. All your friends.'

' "H-h-horses have . . . have . . ." ' They have *four* legs, Dr Merrick.'

'Read the words, Connie!'

'I hate you! I hate all of you!'

'Connie!'

She raced through it. Zap. Two hundred volts. The girl coughed and retched. A coil of thick white mucus shot from her mouth.

'Too much,' gasped Gloria. 'Isn't that too much?'

'You want the treatment to take, don't you?' said Merrick.

'Mommy! Where's my mommy?'

Gloria tore the mike away. 'Right here, dear!'

'Mommy, make them stop!'

'I can't, dear. You must try to be brave.'

The fourth lie arrived. Merrick upped the voltage. 'Read it, lass!'

'No!'

'Read it!'

'Uncle Jack! I want Uncle Jack!'

My throat constricted, my stomach went sour. 'You're doing quite well, Connie,' I said, grabbing the mike. 'I think you'll like your present.'

'Take me home!'

'I got you a pretty nice one.'

Connie balled her face into a mass of wrinkles. ' "Stones"!' she screamed, spitting blood. ' "Are"!' she persisted. ' "Alive"!' She jerked like a gaffed flounder, spasm after spasm. A broad urine stain bloomed on her smock, and despite the mandatory enema a brown fluid dripped from the hem.

'Excellent!' Merrick increased the punishment to three hundred volts. 'The end is in sight, child!'

'No! Please! Please! Enough!' Foam leaked from Connie's mouth.

'You're almost halfway there!'

'Please!'

The tachistoscope kept firing, Connie kept lying: falsehood after falsehood, shock after shock – like a salvo of armed missiles cruising along her nerves, detonating inside her mind. My niece asserted that rats chase cats. She lied about money, saying it grew on trees. The Pope is Jewish, Connie insisted. Grass is purple. Salt is sweet.

As the final lie appeared, she fainted. Even before Gloria could scream, Merrick was inside the glass cell, checking the child's heartbeat. A begrudging admiration seeped through me. The doctor had a job to do, and he did it.

A single dose of ammonium carbonate brought Connie around. Easing her face toward the screen, Merrick turned to me. 'Ready?'

'Huh? You want me . . . ?'

'Hit it when I tell you.'

Reluctantly I rested my finger on the switch. 'I'd rather

not.' True. I wasn't inordinately fond of Connie, but I had no wish to give her pain.

'Read, Connie,' muttered Merrick.

'I c-can't.' Blood and spittle mingled on Connie's chin. 'You all hate me! Mommy hates me!'

'I like you almost as much as I like myself,' said Gloria, leaning over my shoulder. 'You're going to have a satisfactory party.'

'One more, Connie,' I told her. 'Just one more and you'll be a citizen.' The switch felt sharp and hot against my finger. 'A *highly* satisfactory party.'

A single droplet rolled down Connie's cheek, staining it like a trail left by one of Toby's beloved slugs. This was, I realized, the last time she would ever cry. Brainburns did that to you; they drained you of all those destructive and chaotic juices: sentiments, illusions, myths, tears.

' "Dogs can talk",' she said, right before I pierced her heart with alternating current.

And it truly was a highly satisfactory party, filling the entire visitor's lounge and overflowing into the hall. All four of Connie's older sisters came, along with her reading teacher and eight of her girlfriends, half of whom had been cured that month, one on the previous day. They danced the Upright while a compact disc of the newest Probity hit wafted through the ward:

> When skies are grey, and it starts to rain,
> I like to stand by the windowpane,
> And watch each raindrop bounce and fall,
> Then smile, 'cause I'm not getting wet at all.

The hospital supplied the refreshments – a case of Olga's OK Orangeade, a tub of ice cream from No Great Shakes and a slab of chocolate cake the size of a welcome mat. All the girls, I noticed, ate in moderation, letting their ice cream turn to soup. Artificially induced slenderness was, of course, disingenuous, but that was no reason to be a glutton.

The gift-giving ceremony contained one disturbing moment. After opening the expected succession of galoshes, reference books, umbrellas and cambric blouses, Connie unwrapped a fully working model of an amusement park – Happy Land, it was called, complete with roller coaster, ferris wheel and merry-go-round. She blanched, seized by the panic that someone who's just been brainburned invariably feels in the presence of anything electric. Slamming her palm against her lips, she rushed into the bathroom. The friend who'd bought her the Happy Land, a slender, frizzy-haired girl named Beth, reddened with remorse. 'I should've realized,' she moaned.

Was the Happy Land a lie? I wondered. It purported to be an amusement park, but it wasn't.

'I'm so stupid,' whined Beth.

No, I decided, it merely purported to be a replica of an amusement park, which it was.

Connie hobbled out of the bathroom. Silence descended like a sudden snowfall – not the hot snow of a brainburn but the cold, dampening snow of the objective world. Feet were shuffled, throats cleared. The party, obviously, had lost its momentum. Someone said, 'We all had a reasonably good time, Connie,' and that was that.

As her friends and sisters filed out, Connie hugged them with authentic affection (all except Alice Lawrence, whom she evidently didn't like) and offered each a highly personalized thank-you, never forgetting who'd given what. Such a grown-up young lady, I thought. But her greatest display of maturity occurred when I said my own goodbye.

'Take care, Connie.'

'Thanks for coming, Unc, and thanks for the roller skates. Thing is, I already have a pair, better than these. I'll probably swap them for a sweater.'

A citizen now. I was proud of her.

Back at the apartment, the phone-answering machine was blinking. Three flashes, pause, three flashes, pause, three flashes, pause. I grabbed a bottle of Paul's Passable Ale from the fridge and snapped off the top. Three flashes, pause. I took a sizeable swallow. Another. The late-afternoon light poured through the kitchen window and bathed our major appliances in the iridescent orange you see when facing the sun with eyes closed. I finished my beer.

Three flashes, pause, three flashes, pause: a staccato, insistent signal – a cry of distress, I realize in retrospect, like a call beamed semaphorically from a sinking ship.

I pushed PLAY. Toby had written and produced our outgoing message, and he also starred in it: *My folks and I just want to say / We'd like to talk with you today / So speak up when you hear the beep / And we might call back before we sleep.*

Beep, and a harsh male voice zagged into the kitchen. 'Amusing message, sort of – about what I'd expect from a seven-year-old. This is Dr Bamford at the Kraft Institute, and I presume I'm addressing the parents of Toby Sperry. Well, the results are in. The Hob's hare that bit your son was carrying high levels of Xavier's Plague, an uncommon and pathogenic virus. We shipped the specimen to Dr Prendergorst at the Centre for the Palliative Treatment of Hopeless Diseases in Locke Borough. If you have any questions, I'll be only mildly irritated if you call me. From now on, though, the matter is essentially in the Centre's synecdochic hands.' *Beep.* 'John Prendergorst speaking, Centre for the Palliative Treatment of Hopeless Diseases. You've probably heard Bamford's preliminary report by now, and we've just now corroborated it down here at Hopeless. Please call my office at your earliest convenience, and we'll arrange for you to come by and talk, but I'm afraid no amount of talk can change the fact that Xavier's is one hundred per cent fatal. We'll show you the statistics.' *Beep.* 'Hi. It's Helen. I'm at the office, working on that neuropathology of spiritual possession piece. Looks like it'll be a long day and a longer night. There's some chicken in the freezer.'

My reaction was immediate and instinctual. I ran into the study, grabbed Helen's unabridged dictionary and looked up 'fatal', bent on discovering some obscure usage peculiar to Prendergorst's profession. When the doctor said 'fatal', I decided, he didn't mean *fatal*, he meant something far more ambiguous and benign.

25

Fast
Fasten
Fat
Fatal   Adjective. Causing death; mortal; deadly.
Fatalism
Fatality
Fatally

No. The dictionary was lying. Just because Prendergorst's forecast was pessimistic, that didn't make it *true*.

Fata Morgana   Noun. A mirage consisting of multiple images.

And, indeed, a vision now presented itself to my vibrating brain: one of the few copies of *The Journal of Psychic Healing* that I'd elected to spare, a special issue on psycho-neuroimmunology, its cover displaying a pair of radiant hands massaging a human heart.

Fatuous   Adjective. Silly, unreal, illusory.

Psychoneuroimmunology wasn't fatuous, I'd decided – not entirely. Even the peripatetic prose of *The Journal of Psychic Healing* hadn't concealed the scientific validity of cures spawned by the mind-body connection.
So there was hope. Oh, yes, hope. I would scour the city's data banks, I vowed. I would learn about anyone who'd ever beaten a fatal illness by tapping into the obscure powers of his own nervous system. I would tutor myself in sudden remissions, unexpected recoveries and the taxonomy of miracles.

Fault
Faust
Favour
Fawn   Noun. A young deer.

Because, you see, it was like this: on his fifth birthday we'd taken Toby to the Imprisoned Animals Garden in

Spinoza Borough. Fawns roamed the petting zoo at will, prancing about on their cloven hoofs, noses thrust forward in search of hand-outs. Preschoolers swarmed everywhere, feeding the creatures peanut brittle, giggling as the eager tongues stroked their palms. Whenever another person's child laughed upon being so suckled, I was not especially moved. Whenever my own did the same, I felt something else entirely, something difficult to describe.

I believe I saw the alleged God.

3

Appropriately, the Centre for the Palliative Treatment of Hopeless Diseases occupied a terminal location, a rocky promontory extending from the southern end of Locke Borough into the choppy, gunmetal waters of Becket Bay. We arrived at noon on Sunday, Helen driving, me navigating, the map of Veritas spread across my knees, its surface so mottled by rips and holes it seemed to depict the aftermath of a bombing raid. A fanfolded mile of computer paper lay on the back seat, the fruit of my researches into psychoneuroimmunology and the mind-body link. I knew all about miracles now. I was an expert on the impossible.

We parked in the visitors' lot. Tucking the print-out under my arm, I followed Helen across the macadam. The structure looming over us was monumental and menacing, tier upon tier of diminishing concrete floors frosted with grimy stucco, as if Prendergorst's domain were a wedding cake initiating a marriage destined to end in wife abuse and murder.

In the lobby, a stark sign greeted us. ATTENTION: WE REALIZE THE DECOR HERE DOES NOTHING TO AMELIORATE YOUR SORROW AND DESPAIR. WRITE YOUR BOROUGH REPRESENTATIVE. WE'D LIKE TO PUT IN DECENT LIGHTING AND PAINT THE WALLS. A bristle-jawed nurse told us that Dr Prendergorst – 'you'll know him by his eyes, they look like pickled onions' – was expecting us on the eleventh floor.

We entered the elevator, a steamy box crowded with morose men and women, like a cattle boat bearing war refugees from one zone of chaos and catastrophe to another. I reached out to take Helen's hand. The gesture failed. Oiled by sweat, my fingers slipped from her grasp.

No one was waiting in the eleventh floor waiting room, a gloomy niche crammed with overstuffed armchairs and steel engravings of famous cancer victims, a gallery stretching as far back in history as Jonathan Swift. Helen gave our names to the receptionist, a spindly young man with flourishing gardens of acne on his cheeks, who promptly got on the intercom and announced our arrival to Prendergorst, adding, 'They look pale and scared.'

We sat down. Best-selling self-help books littered the coffee table. *You Can Have Somewhat Better Sex. How to Find a Certain Amount of Inner Peace. The Heisenberg Uncertainty Diet.* 'It's a mean system, isn't it?' the receptionist piped up from behind his desk. 'He's in there, you're out here. He seems to matter, you don't. He keeps you waiting – you wait. The whole thing's set up to intimidate you.'

I grunted my agreement. Helen said nothing.

A door opened. A short, round, onion-eyed man in a white lab coat came out, accompanied by a fiftyish couple – a blobby woman in a shabby beige dress and her equally fat, equally dishevelled husband: rumpled golf cap, oversized polyester polo shirt, baggy corduroy pants; they looked like a pair of bookends they'd failed to unload at their own garage sale. 'There's nothing more I can say,' Prendergorst informed them in a low, tepid voice. 'A Hickman catheter is our best move at this point.'

'She's our only child,' said the wife.

'Leukaemia's a tough one,' said Prendergorst.

'Shouldn't you do more tests?' asked the husband.

'Medically – no. But if it would make you feel better . . .'

The couple exchanged terse, pained glances. 'It wouldn't,' said the wife, shambling off.

'True,' said the husband, following.

A minute later we were in Prendergorst's office, Helen and I seated on metal folding chairs, the doctor positioned regally behind a mammoth desk of inlaid cherry. 'Would you like to put some sugar in your brain?' he asked, proffering a box of candy.

'No,' said Helen tonelessly.

'I guess the first step is to confirm the diagnosis, right?' I said, snatching up a dark chocolate nugget. I bit through the outer shell. Brandy trickled into my throat.

'When your son gets back from camp, I'll draw a

29

perfunctory blood sample,' said Prendergorst, sliding an open file folder across his desk. Beneath Toby's name, a gruesome photograph of the deceased Hob's hare lay stapled to the inside front cover, its body reduced by the autopsy to a gutted pelt. 'The specimen they sent us was loaded with the virus,' said the doctor. 'The chances of Toby not being infected are perhaps one in a million.' He whisked the file away, slipping it into his top desk drawer. 'A rabbit killing your child, it's all faintly absurd, don't you think? A snake would make more sense, or a black widow spider, even one of those poisonous toads – can't remember what they're called. But a rabbit . . .'

'So what sort of therapy are we looking at?' I asked. 'I hope it's not too debilitating.'

'We aren't looking at *any* therapy, Mr Sperry. At best, we'll relieve your son's pain until he dies.'

'Toby's only seven,' I said, as if I were a lawyer asking a governor to reprieve an underage client. 'He's only seven years old.'

'I think I'll *sue* that damn camp,' Helen grunted.

'You'd lose,' said Prendergorst, handing her a stark pamphlet, white letters on black paper: *Xavier's Plague and Xavier's-Related Syndrome – The News Is All Bad.* 'I wish I could remember what those toads are called.'

Had my brainburn not purged me of sentimentality and schmaltz, had it not, as it were, atrophied my tear ducts, I think I would have wept right then. Instead I did something almost as unorthodox. 'Dr Prendergorst,' I began, my hands trembling in my lap like two chilly tarantulas, 'I realize that, from your perspective, our son's chances are nil.'

'Quite so.'

I deposited the computer print-out on Prendergorst's desk. 'Look here, over twenty articles from *The Holistic Health Bulletin*, plus the entire *Proceedings of the Eighth Annual Conference on Psychoneuroimmunology* and *The Collected Minutes of the Fifth International Mind-Body Symposium.* Story after story of people thinking their way past heart disease, zapping cancer cells with mental bullets – you name it. Surely you've heard of such cases.'

'Indeed,' said Prendergorst icily.

'Jack . . . *please*,' groaned Helen, wincing with embarrassment. My wife, the *Sweet Reason* reporter.

'Miracles happen,' I persisted. 'Not commonly, not reliably, but they happen.'

'Miracles *happened*,' said Prendergorst, casting a cold eye on the print-out. 'These incidents all come from the Nightmare Era – they're all from the Age of Lies. We're adults now.'

'It's basically a matter of giving the patient a positive outlook,' I explained.

'*Please*,' hissed Helen.

'People can cure themselves,' I asserted.

'I believe it's time we returned to the real world, Mr Sperry.' Prendergorst shoved the print-out away as if it were contaminated with Xavier's. 'Your wife obviously agrees with me.'

'Maybe we should bring Toby home next week,' Helen suggested, fanning herself with the pamphlet. 'The sooner he knows,' she sighed, 'the better.'

Prendergorst slid a pack of Canceroulettes from the breast pocket of his lab coat. 'When's your son scheduled to leave?'

'On the twenty-seventh,' said Helen.

'The symptoms won't start before then. I'd keep him where he is. Why spoil his summer?'

'But he'll be living a lie. He'll go around thinking he's not dying.'

'We *all* go around thinking we're not dying,' said the doctor with a quick little smile. He removed a cigarette, set the pack on the edge of the desk. WARNING: THE SURGEON GENERAL'S CRUSADE AGAINST THIS PRODUCT MAY DISTRACT YOU FROM THE MYRIAD WAYS YOUR GOVERNMENT FAILS TO PROTECT YOUR HEALTH. 'God, what a depraved species we are. I'm telling you Toby is mortally ill, and all the while I'm thinking, "Hey, my life is really pretty good, isn't it? No son of *mine* is dying. Fact is, I take a certain pleasure in these people's suffering." '

'And when the symptoms *do* start?' Helen folded the pamphlet into queer, tortured origami shapes. 'What then?'

31

'Nothing dramatic at first. Headaches, joint pains, some hair loss. His skin may acquire a bluish tint.'

Helen said, 'And then?'

'His lymph nodes will become painful and swollen. His lungs will probably fill with *Pneumocystis carinii*. His temperature —'

'Don't go on,' I said.

The doctor ignited his cigarette. 'Each case is different. Some Xaviers linger for a year, some go in less than a month. In the meantime, we'll do everything we can, which isn't much. Demerol, IV nourishment, antibiotics for the secondary infections.'

'We've heard enough,' I said.

'The worst of it is probably the chills.' Prendergorst took a drag on his cigarette. 'Xaviers, they just can't seem to get warm. We wrap them in electric blankets, and it doesn't make any —'

'Please stop,' I pleaded.

'I'm merely telling the truth,' said the doctor, exhaling a jagged smoke ring.

All the way home, Helen and I said nothing to each other. Nothing about Toby, nothing about Xavier's, nothing about miracles – nothing.

Weirdly, cruelly, my thoughts centred on rabbits. How I would no longer be able to abide their presence in my life. How I would tremble with rage whenever my career required me to criticize a copy of *Peter Rabbit* or an Easter card bearing some grinning bunny. I might even start seeking the animals out, leaving a trail of mysterious, mutilated corpses in my wake, whiskers plucked, ears torn off, tails severed from their rumps and stuffed down their throats.

Total silence. Not one word.

We entered the elevator, pushed *30*. The car made a sudden, rapid ascent, like a pearl diver clambering toward the air: second floor, seventh, twelfth . . .

'How are you feeling?' I said at last.

'Not good,' Helen replied.

' "Not good" – is that all? "Not good"? I feel horrible.'

'In my case, "horrible" would not be a truthful word.'

'I feel all knotted and twisted. Like I'm a glove, and somebody's pulled me inside out' – a bell rang, the numeral *30* flashed above our heads – 'and my vital parts, my heart and lungs, they're naked and—'

'You've been reading too many of the poems you deconstruct.'

'I hate your coldness, Helen.'

'You hate my candour.'

I left the car, started down the hall. Imagined exchanges haunted me – spectral words, ghostly vocables, scenes from an intolerable future.

– Dad, what are these lumps under my arms?

– Swollen lymph nodes, Toby.

– Am I sick, Dad?

– Sicker than you can imagine. You have Xavier's Plague.

– Will I get better?

– No.

– Will I get warm?

– No.

– Will I die?

– Yes.

– What happens when you die, Dad? Do you wake up somewhere else?

– There's no objective evidence for an afterlife, and anecdotal reports of heaven cannot be distinguished from wishful thinking, self-delusion and the effects of oxygen loss on the brain.

The apartment had turned against me. Echoes of Toby were everywhere, infecting the living room like the virus now replicating in his cells – a child-sized boot, a dozen stray chequers, the miniature Crusaders' castle he'd built out of balsa wood the day before he went to camp. 'How do you like it, Dad?' he'd asked as he set the last turret in place. 'It's somewhat ugly,' I'd replied, flinching at the truth. 'It's pretty lopsided,' I'd added, sadly noting the tears welling up in my son's eyes.

On the far wall, the picture window beckoned. I crossed our rugless floor, pressed my palms against the glass. A mile away, a neon sign blazed atop the cathedral in Galileo

33

Square. ASSUMING GOD EXISTS, JESUS MAY HAVE BEEN HIS SON.

Helen went to the bar and made herself a dry martini, flavouring it with four olives skewered on a toothpick like kebabs. 'I wish our son weren't dying,' she said. 'I truly wish it.'

An odd, impossible sentence formed on my tongue. 'Whatever happens, Toby won't learn the truth.'

'Huh?'

'You heard Prendergorst – in the Nightmare Era, terminal patients sometimes tapped their bodies' natural powers of regeneration. It's all a matter of attitude. If Toby believes there's hope, he might have a remission.'

'But there isn't any hope.'

'Maybe.'

'There *isn't*.'

'I'll go to him and I'll say, "Buddy, soon the doctors will ... the doctors, any day now, they'll ... they'll c-c ..." '

Cure you – but instead my conditioning kicked in, a hammerblow in my skull, a hot spasm in my chest.

'I know the word, Jack. Stop kidding yourself. It's uncivilized to carry on like this.' Helen sipped her martini. 'Want one?'

'No.'

I fixed on the metropolis, its bright towers and spangled skyscrapers rising into a misty, starless night. Within my disordered brain, a plan was taking shape, as palpable as any sculpture I'd ever deconstructed at the Wittgenstein.

'They're out there,' I said.

'Who?'

'They can lie. And maybe they can teach *me* to lie.'

'You're talking irrationally, Jack. I wish you wouldn't talk irrationally.'

It was all clear now. 'Helen, I'm going to become one of them – I'm going to become a dissembler.' I pulled my hand away, leaving my palm imprinted on the glass like a fortune teller's logo. 'And then I'm going to convince Toby he has a chance.'

'I don't think that's a very good idea.'

'Somehow they've gotten around the burn. And if *they* can, *I* can.'

Helen lifted the toothpick from her martini glass and sucked the olives into her mouth. 'Toby's hair will start shedding in two weeks. He's certain to ask what that means.'

Two weeks. Was that all I had? 'I'll say it means n-n-nothing.' A common illness, I'd tell him. A disease easily licked.

'Jack – *don't.*'

A mere two weeks. A feeble fourteen days.

I ran to the kitchen, snatched up the phone. I need to see you, I'd tell her. This isn't about sex, Martina.

610–400.

It rang three times, then came a distant click, ominous and hollow. 'The number you have reached,' ran the recorded operator in a harsh, gravelly voice, 'is out of service.' My bowels became as hard and cold as a glacier. 'Probably an unpaid bill,' the taped message continued. 'We're pretty quick to disconnect in such cases.'

'Out of service,' I told Helen.

'Good,' she said.

7 Lacklustre Lane, Descartes Borough.

Helen polished off her martini. 'Now let's forget this ridiculous notion,' she said. 'Let's face the future with honesty, clearheadedness and . . .'

But I was already out the door.

Girding the grey and oily Pathogen River, Lacklustre Lane was alive with smells: scum, guano, sulphur, methane, decaying eels – a cacophony of stench blaring through the shell of my Adequate. 'And, of course, at the centre of my opposition to abortion,' said the sombre priest on my car radio, 'is my belief that sex is a fundamentally disgusting practice to begin with.' This was the city's frankest district, a mass of defunct fishmarkets and abandoned warehouses piled together like dead cells waiting to be sloughed off. 'You might even say that, like many of my ilk, I have an instinctive horror of the human body.'

And suddenly there it was, Number 7, a corrugated tin shanty sitting on a cluster of pylons rising from the Pathogen like mortally ill trees. Gulls swung through the summer air, dropping their guileless excrement on the dock; water lapped against the moored hull of a houseboat, the *Average Josephine* – a harsh, sucking sound, as if a pride of invisible lions were drinking there. I pulled over.

A series of narrow, jackknifing gangplanks rose from the nearest pier like a sliding board out of *The Cabinet of Dr Caligari* – one of my most memorable forays into film criticism – eventually reaching the landing outside Martina's door. I climbed. I knocked. Nothing. I knocked again, harder. The door drifted open.

I called, 'Martina?'

The place had been stripped, emptied out like the Hob's hare whose photo I'd seen that morning in Prendergorst's office. The front parlour contained a crumpled beer can, a mousetrap baited with calcified cheddar, some cigarette butts – and nothing else. I went to the kitchen. The sink held a malodorous broth of water, soap, grease and cornflakes. The shelves were empty.

'Martina? Martina?'

In the back room, a naked set of rusting bedsprings sat on a pinewood frame so crooked it might have come from Toby's workshop.

I returned to the hot, sour daylight, paused on Martina's landing. A wave of nausea rolled through me, straight to my putative soul.

Out on the river, a Brutality Squad cutter bore down on an outboard motorboat carrying two men in green ponchos. Evidently they were attempting to escape – every paradise· will have its dissidents, every utopia its defectors – an ambition abruptly thwarted as a round of machine-gun fire burst from the cutter, killing both fugitives instantly. Their corpses fell into the Pathogen, reddening it like dye markers. I felt a quick rush of qualified sympathy. Such fools. Didn't they know that for most intents and a majority of purposes Veritas was as good as it gets?

'Some people . . .'

I looked toward the dock. A tall, fortyish, excruciatingly thin man in hip boots and a tattered white sweatshirt stood on the foredeck of *Average Josephine*.

'. . . Are so naive,' he continued. 'Imagine, trying to run the channel in broad daylight.' He reached through a hole in his shirt and scratched his hairy chest. 'Your girlfriend's gone.'

'Are you referring to Martina Coventry?' I asked.

'Uh-huh.'

'She's not my girlfriend.'

'The little synecdochic cunt owes me two hundred dollars in rent.'

I descended through the maze of gangplanks. 'You're her landlord?'

'Mister, in my wretched life I've acquired three things of value – this houseboat, that shanty and my good name.' Martina's landlord stomped his boot on the deck. He had an extraordinarily chaotic and unseemly beard, like a bird's nest constructed under a bid system. 'You know how much a corporation vice president typically pulls down in a month? Twelve thousand. I'm lucky to see that in a *year*. Clamming's a pathetic career.'

'Clamming?'

'Well, you can't make a living renting out a damn shanty, that's for sure,' said Martina's landlord. 'Of course, you can't make one clamming either. You from the Squad? Is Coventry wanted by the law?'

'I'm not from the Squad.'

'Good.'

'But I have to find her. It's vital.' I approached within five feet of the landlord. He smelled like turtle food. 'Can you give me any leads?'

'Not really. Want some clam chowder? I raked 'em up myself.'

'You seem like a highly unsanitary person. How do I know your chowder won't make me ill?'

He smiled, revealing a severe shortage of teeth. 'You'll have to take your chances.'

And that's how I ended up in the snug galley of *Average Josephine*, savouring the best clam chowder I'd ever eaten.

His name was Boris – Boris the Clamdigger – and he knew almost as little about Martina as I did. They'd had sex once, in lieu of the rent. Afterwards, he'd read some of her doggerel, and thought it barely suitable for equipping an outhouse. Evidently she'd been promised a job writing greeting-card verses for Cloying and Coy: they'd reneged; she'd run out of cash; she'd fled in panic.

' "Vital",' Boris muttered. 'You said "vital", and I can tell from your sad eyes, which are a trifle beady, a minor flaw in your moderately handsome face – I can tell "vital" was exactly what you meant. It's a heavy burden you're carrying around, something you'd rather not discuss. Don't worry, Jack, I won't pry. You see, I rather like you, even though you probably make a lot of money. How much do you make?'

I stared at my chowder, lumpy with robust clams and bulbous potatoes. 'Two thousand a month.'

'I *knew* it,' said Boris. 'Of course, that's *nothing* next to what a real estate agent or a borough rep pulls down. What field?'

'Art criticism.'

'I've got to get out of clams. I've got to get out of *Veritas*, actually – a dream I don't mind sharing with somebody who's not a Squad officer. It's a big planet, Jack. One day I'll just pull up anchor and *whoosh* – I'm gone.'

The shock and indignation I should have felt at such perverse musings would not come. 'Boris, do you believe in miracles?' I asked.

'There are times when I don't believe in anything else. How's the chowder?'

'Terrific.'

'I know.'

'Want some more?'

'Sure.'

'I don't see how you'd ever escape,' I said. 'The Squad would shoot you down.'

'Probably.' My host swallowed a large spoonful of his exquisite chowder. 'At least I'd be getting out of clams.'

4

Monday: back to work, my flesh like lead, my blood like liquid mercury. I'd spent the previous week locked in the Wittgenstein's tiny screening room, scrutinizing the fruit of Hollywood's halcyon days and confirming the archaeologists' suspicions that these narratives contained not one frame of truth, and now it was time to deconstruct them, *Singin' in the Rain*, *Doctor Zhivago*, *Rocky*, the whole deceiving lot. Hour followed hour, day melded into day, but my routine never varied: filling the bathtubs, dumping in the 35mm negatives, watching the triumph of Clorox over illusion. Like souls leaving bodies, the Technicolor emulsions floated free of their bases, disintegrating in the potent, purifying bleach.

My heart wasn't in it. Cohn, Warner, Mayer, Thalberg, Selznick – these men were not my enemies. *Au contraire*, I wanted to be like them; I wanted to *be* them. Whatever one might say against Hollywood's moguls, they could all have blessed their ailing children with curative encouragement and therapeutic falsehoods.

Stanley Marcus stayed away until Thursday, when he suddenly appeared in my coffee cubicle as I was dispiritedly consuming a tuna-fish sandwich and attempting, without success, to drown my sorrows in caffeine. Saying nothing, he took up his broom and swept the floor with slow, morose strokes.

'That recommendation letter was pretty nasty,' he said at last, sweating in the July heat. 'I wish you hadn't called me a toady.'

'I had a choice?'

'I didn't get the promotion.'

'It's not easy for me to pity you,' I said through a mouthful of tuna, mayo and Respectable Rye. 'I have a sick son. Only lies can cure him.'

Stanley rammed his broom into the floor. 'Look, I'm a

40

ridiculous person, we all know that. Women want nothing to do with me. I'm a loner. Don't talk to me about your home life, Mr Sperry. Don't talk about your lousy son.'

I blanched and trembled. 'Fuck you figuratively, Stanley Marcus!'

'Fuck *you* figuratively, Jack Sperry!' He clutched the broom against his bosom, pivoted on his heel and fled.

I finished my coffee and decided to make some more, using a double helping of crystals from my Donaldson's Drinkable jar.

Back in the shop, yet another stack of 35mm reels awaited my review, a celluloid tower stretching clear to the ceiling. As Donaldson's Drinkable cavorted, so to speak, through my neurons, I rolled up my sleeves and got to work. I dissolved *The Wizard of Oz* and *Gone With the Wind*, stripped *Citizen Kane* and *King Kong* down to the acetate, rid the world of *Top Hat*, *A Night at the Opera*, and – how blatant can a prevaricator get? – *It's a Wonderful Life*.

The end-of-day whistle blew, a half-dozen steamy squeals echoing throughout the Wittgenstein. As the last cry faded away, a seventh one arose, human, female – familiar.

'Way to go, critic!'

I glanced up from my tub of Clorox, where *Casablanca* was currently burbling toward oblivion. The doorway framed her.

'Martina? *Martina?*'

'Hello, Jack.' Her silver lamé dress hugged her every contour like some elaborate skin graft. A matching handbag swung from her shoulder. I'd never seen a Veritasian outfitted so dishonestly before – but then, of course, Martina was evidently much more than a Veritasian.

'The guard let you through?' I asked, astonished.

'After I agreed to copulate with him tomorrow, yes.'

The truth? A half-truth? There was no way, I realized with a sudden pang of anxiety, to gauge this woman's sincerity. 'I'm extraordinarily happy to see you,' I said. 'I went to that address you gave me, but—'

'Just *once* I'd like to meet a man whose genitalia didn't rule his life.'

41

'I wanted to talk with you, that's all. A *talk*. I met Boris the Clamdigger.'

Opening her silver handbag, Martina retrieved a one-litre bottle of Charlie's Cheapdrunk and a pair of Styrofoam cups. 'Did he mention anything about two hundred bucks?'

'Uh-huh.'

'He's not going to get it.' She set the cups on my workbench and filled them with mud-coloured wine. 'I suppose he told you we had sex?'

'Yes.'

'Hell, Jack, you know more about my private life than *I* do.' She seized her cup of Charlie's and sashayed around the shop, breasts rolling like channel buoys on Becket Bay, hips swaying like mounds of dough being hefted by a pizza chef.

It was all lost on me, every bounce and bob. My urges had died when Prendergorst said *fatal*; I'd been gelded by an adjective.

Grabbing my wine, I swilled it down in one gulp.

'So this is where it all happens.' Martina stopped before my tool rack, massaging my axes, fondling my tin snips, running her fingers over my saws, pliers and drills. 'Impressive . . .'

'Where are you living now?' I asked, refilling my cup.

'With my girlfriend. I can't afford anything better – Cloying and Coy turned down my Mother's Day series.' She finished off her Charlie's. 'Which reminds me – you know that page of doggerel I gave you?'

Like a chipmunk loading up on acorns, I inflated my cheeks with wine. I swallowed. 'Those verses have never left my mind. As it were.'

Martina frowned severely, apparently puzzled by the notion that her doggerel was in any way memorable. 'I want them back. You never liked them in the first place.'

The wine was everywhere now, warming my hands and feet, massaging my brain. 'They're somewhat appealing, in their own vapid way.'

Hips in high gear, she moved past the seething remains of *Casablanca*, reached the door and snapped the deadbolt into place. 'I don't know what I was thinking when I let them go. I always save my original manuscripts. I'll gladly give you a copy.'

So there it was, the final proof of Martina's true colours. The cunning little liar had deduced the poems were dangerous – in her justified paranoia, she'd imagined me spotting the flagrant falsehoods embedded in the page.

Buzzing with Cheapdrunk, I didn't resist when Martina ushered me across the shop to my assignment for the upcoming week – a mountainous pile of Cassini gowns, Saint Laurent shirts and Calvin Klein jeans.

'So anyway,' she said as we eased into the fraudulent fabrics, 'if you could give me those verses . . .'

Her full wet lips came toward me, her eager puppyish tongue emerged. She kissed me all over; it was like being molested by a marshmallow. We hugged and fondled, clutched and tussled, poked and probed.

My genitalia, to use Martina's word, might as well have been on the moon, for all they cared. I said, 'Martina, I know why you want that doggerel.'

'Oh?'

Icy vibrations passed through her, the tremors of her guilt. 'You want it because the paper's riddled with lies,' I said. The skin tightened on her bones. 'You're a dissembler.'

'No,' she insisted, extricating herself from our embrace.

'How do you counteract the conditioning?' I persisted.

She stood up. 'I'm *not* one.'

'You wrote about having wings. You wrote about a *soul*.' Scrambling to my feet, I squeezed her large, Rubensian hand. 'My son means a great deal to me. Love, even. He's just a boy. Ever heard of Xavier's Plague? He mustn't learn the truth. If he doesn't realize it's fatal, he might go into remission or even—'

She ran to the door as if fleeing some act of the alleged God, a forest fire, tidal wave, cyclone. 'You've got the wrong woman!' she shouted, throwing back the bolt.

'I won't go to the Squad – I promise. Please, Martina, teach me how you do it!'

She tore open the door, started into the hot dusk. 'I tell only the truth!'

'Liar!'

Sweating and shaking, she fumbled into her shiny Toyota Functional and backed out of the parking lot. Her rubbery face was bloodless. Her eyes flashed with fear. Martina Coventry: dissembler. Oh, yes, truer words had never been spoken.

She will not escape, I silently vowed, clasping my hands together in that most dangerous of postures and disingenuous of gestures. *With God as my witness*, I added with a nod to the late, great *Gone With the Wind*.

Heaven answered me with a traffic jam, the full glory of the Veritasian rush hour. I ran into its dense screeching depths, weaving around pedestrians like a skier following a slalom course, never letting Martina's Perfunctory out of my sight. She crawled down Voltaire Avenue, turned east onto River Lane. By the time she reached the bridge, the traffic had halted completely, like a wave of molten lava solidifying on the slope of a volcano.

She pulled into a parking space, started the meter and ducked into a seedy-looking bar-and-grill called Dolly's Digestibles.

A pay telephone stood at the Schopenhauer Avenue intersection. The thing worked perfectly. In the Age of Lies, I'd heard, public phones were commonly the targets of criminal behaviour.

I told Helen I wouldn't be home for supper. 'I'm tracking a dissembler,' I explained.

'The Coventry woman?'

'Yes.' I peered through the bar's grubby window. Martina sat in the back, sipping an Olga's OK Orangeade and eating a murdered cow.

Helen said, 'Did you have sex with her?'

'No.' A mild but undeniable pain arose in my temples. 'We kissed.'

'On the lips?'

'Yes. We also hugged.'

'Come home, Jack.'

'Not before I'm one of them.'

'Jack!'

Click. I stood in the silvery, sulphurous rain and waited.

*

Within the hour Martina left Dolly's Digestibles and set out on foot, striding eastward into the twilit depths of Nietzsche Borough. Once the lynchpin of the Veritas Trolley Company, an enterprise that in its heyday shuttled both freight and humans around the metropolis, Nietzsche had of late fallen victim to the revolution in private transportation, becoming underpopulated and inert, an urban moonscape. I followed Martina to a depot, its tracks now deserted but for the occasional rusting Pullman or decaying boxcar. How stealthy I was, how furtive – how like a dissembler already.

A roundhouse loomed up, its turntable lying before the switchyard like an enormous lazy Susan, its barns sealed with slabs of corrugated steel. A diesel switch engine sat on the nearest siding, hulking into the wet summer air like the fossilized remains of some postindustrial dinosaur.

Martina drummed on the door – a swift, snappy paradiddle – and a tall, devil-bearded man answered, his gaunt features softened by the dusk. 'I'm Spartacus, come to free the slaves,' she told him – a code phrase, evidently. I flinched at the falsehood.

'This way, brave Thracian,' he replied, stepping aside to let her pass.

Sneaking around back, I groped along the sooty, rust-stained walls. A high, open window beckoned. I was all instinct now, piling the handiest junk together (pickle barrel, apple crate, fifty-five-gallon drum), scrambling upward like the hero of some Cinemascope illusion. I reached the sill and peered in.

Liars – everywhere, liars. There were over four hundred of them, chattering among themselves as they gripped kerosene lanterns and drifted amid the empty rails, gradually converging upon a makeshift wooden podium suspended several feet above the ground on stilts. The women were dressed outrageously, in low-cut sequined blouses and spangled stretch pants, like chorus girls out of a Fred Astaire movie; Martina fit right in. The men's attire was equally antisocial. They wore tuxedos with white gloves; riding cloaks and jodhpurs; lavender suits that might have been stolen from pimps.

A burly man in a zoot suit mounted the steps of the

podium, carrying a battery-powered bullhorn. 'Settle down, everybody!' came his electrified bellow.

The mob grew quiet. 'Take it away, Sebastian!' somebody called from the floor.

The liars' leader – Sebastian – strutted back and forth on the podium, flashing a jack-o'-lantern grin. 'What is snow?' he shouted.

I fixed on Martina. 'Snow is hot!' she screamed along with her peers.

A dull ache wove through my belly. I closed my eyes and jumped into the thick, creosote-clogged air.

'What chases cats?' Sebastian demanded.

'Rats chase cats!' the liars responded in a single voice – a mighty shout drowning out the thud of my boots striking the roundhouse floor. *Rats chase cats*: God. My discomfort increased, nausea pounding deep within me. I backed against a rivet-studded girder, my body camouflaged by shadows, my footfalls masked by the rumble of the crowd.

'Now,' said Sebastian, 'down to business . . .'

Gradually the sickness passed, and I was able to monitor the schemes now unfolding before me.

The dissemblers – I quickly learned – were planning yet another attack on Veritas's domestic tranquillity. For one astonishingly disruptive afternoon, they would revive what Sebastian called 'that vanished and miraculous festival known as Christmas'. Anything to demoralize the city, evidently, anything to rot it from within. At 2 p.m. on 25 December, when Circumspect Park was packed with families out for a jolly afternoon of skating on the duck pond and drinking hot chocolate by bonfires, the liars would strike. Costumed as angels, elves, gnomes and sugarplum fairies, they would swoop into the park and cordon it off with snow fences, discreetly taking a dozen hostages to discourage police intervention. Sebastian's forces would next erect a so-called Christmas tree on the north shore of the pond – a Scotch pine as big as a windmill – immediately inviting Veritas's presumably awestruck children to decorate it with glass balls and tinsel. Then, as evening drew near, the dissemblers would perform a three-act adaptation of a Charles Dickens story called *A Christmas Carol*. I knew all

47

about that story, and not just because I'd read a copy of the first edition prior to burning it. *A Christmas Carol* had entered history as one of the falsest fables of all time, a glib embodiment of the lie that the wicked can be made to see the errors of their ways.

Finally: the climax. A loading gantry would appear on the scene and suddenly – look – here comes old Santa Claus himself, descending from the sky in a shiny red sleigh harnessed to eight audio-animatronic reindeer and jammed with gifts wrapped in glittery gold paper. As the children gathered around – their hearts pounding with delight, their faces aglow with glee, their poor defenceless minds dizzy with delusion – the elves would shower them with the stuff of their dreams, with scooters and ten-speeds, doll houses and electric trains, teddy bears and toy soldiers.

Sebastian held up the red suit, pillow and fake beard he intended to wear as Santa Claus, and the roundhouse broke into instant, thunderous applause.

I studied the crowd, shuddering each time I came upon a familiar face. Good heavens: Jimmy Breeze, the bartender from Booze Before Breakfast. Who would have picked *him* for a liar? Or my plumber, Paul Irving? Or my barber, Bill Mumford?

Sebastian divided his legions into the necessary task forces. Jimmy Breeze ended up on the Ornaments Committee; my plumber was cast as Ebenezer Scrooge; my barber volunteered to be an elf; Martina agreed to write Santa's opening oration.

The closing litany caught me by surprise.

'What can dogs do?' Sebastian shouted abruptly.

'They can talk!' answered the mob.

My skull began to throb.

'What colour is grass?'

'Purple!'

The pounding in my skull intensified.

'Stones are . . .'

'Alive!'

'Stop!' I cried, squeezing my head between my palms. 'Stop! Please stop!'

Four hundred faces turned toward me. Eight hundred eyes blazed with anger and indignation.

'Who's that?' someone asked.

'Spy!' a voice called.

Another voice: 'Brutality Squad!'

Another: 'Get him!'

I raised my open palms. 'Listen! I want to join you!' The liars rushed toward me like the hordes in the most impressive Renaissance oil I'd deconstructed during my apprenticeship, Altdorfer's *Battle of Issus*. 'I want to become a dissembler!'

A leathery hand curled around my mouth. I bit into it, tasting the liar's salty blood. A boot jabbed my side, snapping one of my ribs like a dry twig. Groaning, reeling with fear, I dropped to my knees. I'd never before felt so much of that ultimate truth, that quintessential fact, pain.

The last thing I saw before losing consciousness was my tax advisor's fist moving swiftly toward my jaw.

I woke up alive. Alive – and no better. My lips felt like two fat snails grafted onto my mouth. My torso, it seemed, had recently been employed as the ball in some obscure and violent contact sport. Pain chewed at my side.

Gradually the gooey film slid from my eyes. I took stock. Foam mattress, eiderdown pillow, the adamant odour of rubbing alcohol. Adhesive tape encircled my chest, as if it were the gripping end of a baseball bat.

A middle-aged doctor in a white lab coat fidgeted beside me, stethoscope dangling from her neck. 'Good morning,' she said, apparently meaning it. A thin, vivid face – beaky nose, sharp chin, high cheeks: a face that, while not beautiful, would probably always retain a certain fascination for anybody obliged to behold it regularly.

'Morning? Is it Friday already?'

'Very good,' the doctor answered merrily. Her smile was as crisp and bright as a gibbous moon. 'I'm Felicia Krakower, and I truly, sincerely hope you're feeling better.'

Across the room, an old man with skin the colour of oolong tea sat upright on his mattress, his head wrapped in a turban of brilliant white bandages.

'My rib hurts,' I said.

'I'm terribly sorry to hear that,' said Dr Krakower. 'Don't fret. You're in Satirev now.'

'Satirev?'

'Off the map.' Dr Krakower waved a thermometer around as if conducting an orchestra.

'Spell it backwards,' my roommate suggested. 'I'm Louie, by the way. Brain cancer. No big deal. It just grows and grows up there, like moss, and then one day – pfttt – I'm gone. Death is an extraordinary adventure.'

I slid the thermometer between my lips. Satirev . . . Veritas . . . Satirev . . . Veritas . . .

My accommodations were coated with lurid yellow paint and equally lurid lies – a poster-sized edition of Keats's 'Ode on a Grecian Urn', a reproduction of Van Gogh's *Sunflowers*, a print of Salvador Dali's notorious landscape of trees fruited with pocket watches. I glanced through a rose-tinted window. Outside, a rank of Corinthian columns supported a carved lintel reading CENTRE FOR CREATIVE WELLNESS.

As Felicia Krakower removed the thermometer, I pressed my staved-in side and said, 'Doctor, you've heard of psychoneuroimmunology, haven't you?'

'The mind-body connection?'

'Right. The patient adopts such a cheerful outlook that his sickness never takes hold. Does that ever happen?'

'Of *course* it happens,' the doctor replied, sliding her index finger along the bright yellow tubing of her stethoscope. 'Miracles happen every day – the sun comes up, a baby gets born – and don't you ever forget it, Jack Sperry.'

How marvellous to be among people who weren't afraid of hope. 'Bless you, doctor – am I running a fever?'

'Maybe a tiny one. Not to worry. In Satirev, one never stays ill for long.'

'I should call my wife.'

Against all odds, the doctor's smile grew even larger. 'You have a *wife?* Wonderful. Lovely. I'll relay your request to Internal Security immediately. Open your mouth, would you?'

'Why?'

'Something for your own good.'

I moved my wounded lips apart. The doctor deposited a sugary, kidney-shaped capsule on my tongue, handed me a glass of water. 'How do I *know* it's for my own good?'

'Trust me,' said Dr Krakower.

'In Satirev people trust each other,' said Louie.

'Sleeping pill?' I asked, swallowing.

'Could be,' said the doctor.

Sleeping pill . . .

When I returned to awareness, Martina Coventry was leaning over me, still packaged in her lascivious silver dress. Beside her stood a tall, lanky, coarse-skinned man in a green dinner jacket fitted over a sweatshirt that said, WHEN LIFE GIVES YOU LEMONS, MAKE LEMONADE. He looked like a cactus.

'Martina!'

She laid a plump hand on my forehead. 'Say hello to Franz Beauchamp.'

'Hello,' I said to the cactoid man.

'I'm in charge of making sure you don't wander off,' Franz explained in a voice that seemed to enter the room after first travelling through a vat of honey. 'It's no big deal. Just give me your Veritasian word you won't wander off.'

'I won't wander off.'

'Good for you.' My guardian's grin was as spectacular as Felicia Krakower's; I'd fallen in with a community of smilers. 'I have a feeling we're going to be great friends,' he said.

Martina was gaudier than ever. She'd worked her terra-cotta hair into a sculpted object, a thick braid that lay on her shoulder like a loaf of challah. Her eyes had become cartoons of themselves, boldly outlined and richly shaded. 'Even though this is Satirev,' she said, 'I am Veritasian enough to speak frankly. I saved your ass, Jack. You're alive because good old Martina Coventry argued your case back at the roundhouse.'

'I'm grateful,' I said.

'You should be.'

'You told them about Toby?'

51

She nodded. 'Yes, and I must say, the story was an instant hit. A Xavier's child with a shot at remission – you have no idea what appeal that sort of situation holds down here.'

'It's all so amazingly touching,' said Franz. 'A father fighting for his son's life – my *goodness*, that's touching.'

'Can you teach me to lie?' I asked.

'It depends,' said Martina.

'On what?'

'On whether you're accepted into the programme – on whether the treatment takes. Not everyone has the stuff to become a dissembler.'

'It it were up to me, I'd let you in' – Franz snapped his fingers – 'like *that*.'

'Unfortunately, it's not up to us,' said Martina. 'You're going to need some luck.' She reached into her madras bag and took out, of all things, a horseshoe. She opened the drawer in my nightstand and dropped it in, *thud*. 'Horses have six legs,' she said, matter-of-factly.

I gritted my teeth. 'Good luck charms are lies,' I countered.

'Perhaps,' said Martina.

'I understand you wish to make a phone call,' said Franz brightly. 'Speaking on behalf of Internal Security, I must tell you we're *delighted* to grant that particular request.'

Franz and Martina helped me to my feet, inch by painful inch. I'd never realized I owned so many vulnerable muscles, so many assaultable bones. At last I stood, the cold floor nipping at my bare feet, my baggy and absurdly short hospital gown brushing my rump.

The Centre for Creative Wellness was a modest affair. A dozen paces down a hall hung with photographs of ecstatic children, a dozen more across a lobby loaded with Monet's paintings of water lilies, and suddenly we were moving through the main entrance and into a small private park. Graffiti coated the smooth brick walls: JESUS LOVES YOU . . . EVERYTHING IS BEAUTIFUL IN ITS OWN WAY . . . TODAY IS THE FIRST DAY OF THE REST OF YOUR LIFE. I looked up. No sun, no clouds – no sky. The whole park was covered by a concrete arch suggesting the vaulted dome of a cathedral; three mercury-vapour searchlights lay suspended from the roof, technological suns.

'We're under the ground,' Martina explained, noting the confusion on my face. 'We're under Veritas,' she said, launching her index finger upward; her nails were painted a fluorescent green. 'So far we've colonized only a hundred acres, but we're expanding all the time.'

Compact, enclosed – and yet the park was not claustrophobic. Indeed, I had never before stood in such a soothing and airy space. It smelled of pine sap. The omnipresent birdsong boasted the exhilarating intricacy of a fugue. Butterflies representing a dozen species, each more colourful than the next, fluttered about like patches attempting to fuse themselves into a crazy quilt. A flagstone footpath meandered amid neat little gardens planted with zinnias, gladioli, tulips and peonies.

Martina said, 'We'll never grow as big as Veritas, of course. But that's not the point.'

I studied the roof, its curving face crisscrossed with Veritas's innards – her concrete intestines, gushing lead veins, buzzing nerves of steel and gutta-percha. Something peculiar glided over my head.

'The point is that Satirev is here,' Martina continued, 'and that it works.'

A pig. A *pig*? Yes, there it was, sailing through the air like a miniature dirigible, flapping its little cherub-wings. A machine of some kind, a child's bizarre toy? No, its squeal was disconcertingly organic.

'Pigs have wings,' said Franz. His lie sent a chill through my flesh.

A scrawny yellow cat sidled out from behind a forsythia bush, its hairs erect with feline anxiety. It shaped itself into an oblong of fur and shot toward the Centre for Creative Wellness. An instant later, its pursuer appeared. A dog, I assumed at first. But no. Wrong shape. And that tail, long and ropelike.

The shudder began in my lower spine and expanded. A rat. A rat the size of a pregnant badger.

Chasing a cat.

'This is a very strange place,' I said, staring into Martina's exotically adorned eyes. 'Wouldn't you say?'

'Strangeness is relative,' she replied.

'I'm bewildered,' I said.

'It's not hard to make a lie. Avant-garde microbiology will give you a flying pig, an outsized rat – anything you want.'

'I'm *still* bewildered.'

'Satirev takes some getting used to,' said Franz, smiling prolifically. 'I'm sure you'll be able to master it. You look like a champ to me, Jack.'

The telephone booth sat on a knoll smothered in purple grass and five-leaf clovers. Slowly I limped through the odd flora – my body felt like a single gigantic bruise – and pushed the sliding door against the jamb. Martina and Franz stood beside me, well within earshot.

'Do you understand how you must conduct yourself?' my guardian asked.

'I think so.'

'Drop the slightest hint and, bang, you're back in Veritas, awash in scopolamine – you'll never remember you've been here, not one detail. That would be most unfortunate, wouldn't it?'

The phone was a deceitful affair, secretly wired into the Veritas system, blatantly looting its services. I extended my index finger, pressed the appropriate buttons.

Helen didn't answer till the seventh ring. Obviously I'd awakened her. 'Hello?' she said groggily.

'Did I wake you?'

'Of *course* you woke me,' she mumbled, 'whoever you are.'

'Listen,' I told her abruptly. 'Don't ask me anything.'

'*Jack?* Is that *you?*'

'It's me. Don't ask me where I am, Helen. Everything depends on it.'

My wife exhaled in frustration. 'I . . . er, it's good to hear your voice, Jack.'

'I'm among them. Do you know what I'm talking about?'

'I think so.'

'They're considering my case, Helen. They might let me in. I hope you're not still against me on this.'

'I'm against you,' she grunted.

I looped the phone cord around my arm, forcing it tight against my skin like a phylactery strap. 'Have you heard anything from Toby?'

'Postcard came today.'

'Did he mention his health – joint pains or anything?'

'He simply said he was in a canoe race. I'm supposed to pick him up at the bus station on the twenty-seventh.'

'Nothing about headaches?'

'No.'

I kissed the plastic mouthpiece. 'I'll call you back as soon as I can. Goodbye, Helen. I'm terribly fond of you.'

'I'm terribly fond of you too, Jack – but please get out of there. *Please*.'

I hung up and turned toward Martina and Franz. Behind them, a shaggy black rat pinned a Siamese cat to the ground and began tearing out its throat.

'You did fine,' said my guardian.

5

The weather engineers had just turned up their rheostats, flooding the Saturday morning sky with a dazzling emerald sunrise, when Martina came bouncing into my hospital room. She opened the drawer of my nightstand and removed her ludicrous horseshoe. 'It worked,' she insisted, holding out the shoe as if it were a wishbone we'd agreed to split.

'Oh?' I said sneeringly, sceptically: I refused to descend into superstition – psychoneuroimmunology was for real.

She dropped the horseshoe into her handbag. I was lucky, she told me. The typical supplicant was commonly sequestered for a full month in the Hotel Paradise while the government decided his fate – but not I. Instead, assuming Dr Krakower agreed to release me, I would meet that very afternoon with Manny Ginsburg himself.

'Imagine, Jack – you've been granted an audience with the Pope!'

Twenty minutes later Dr Krakower appeared, accompanied by the eternally unctuous Franz Beauchamp. As Martina looked on with seemingly genuine concern, Franz with a kind of smarmy pity, the doctor inspected my infirmities. She removed the bandage from my head wound, palpated my broken rib through the adhesive tape – 'This might hurt a bit,' she warned before sending me into paroxysms of pain – and cheerily pronounced me fit to travel, though she wanted me back by sundown for another checkup.

I got into the denim overalls I'd worn to work on Thursday: how far away that Thursday seemed, how remote and unreal. Martina and Franz guided me through the hospital lobby and across the park to the banks of a wide canal labelled *Jordan River*, its waters clean, clear and redolent of some happy mixture of root beer and maple syrup. Golden trout flashed beneath the surface like reflected moonbeams.

Sparkling with fresh paint, a red gondola lay moored to the wharf. We got on board. As my guardian poled us forward, pushing his oar into the sweet waters, Martina briefed me on the intricacies of dealing with Pope Manny.

'To begin with, he's a year-rounder. Lives here all the time.' For most dissemblers, Martina elaborated, Satirev was a pied-à-terre, locus of the periodic pilgrimages through which one renewed one's talent for mendacity, whereas Manny Ginsburg never left. 'It's made him a little nuts,' she explained.

'I'm not surprised,' I said as an aquatic ferret leaped out of the Jordan and snatched an unsuspecting polka-dotted frog from the shore.

'Play up your devotion to your kid,' Martina advised. 'How you'd move heaven and earth to cure him. The man likes sentiment.'

'And don't look him in the eye,' said Franz. 'He hates directness.'

My guardian landed us at a trim, sturdy, immaculately whitewashed dock, its pilings decorated with ceramic replicas of pelicans and sea gulls. An equally clean and appealing structure rose from the shore – a bait shack or possibly a fisherman's hut. A German shepherd sprawled on the welcome mat, head bobbing in languid circles as it tracked a dragonfly.

'The Holy See,' said Martina, pointing.

'It's a bait shack,' I corrected her.

'It's the Holy See,' said Franz as he lashed his gondola to the dock.

'Maybe we don't have the budget we'd like around here,' said the dog, 'but it's still the Holy See.'

I didn't bat an eye. I was getting used to this sort of thing.

The door swished open on well-oiled hinges, and a short, nervous, wall-eyed man in his sixties ambled onto the dock wearing a brilliant white polyester suit and a yarmulke. He told Martina and Franz to come back for me in an hour.

'Care for a cup of fresh-perked coffee?' asked Manny

57

Ginsburg as he led me into his one-room riverfront abode. The German shepherd followed, claws clicking on the wooden floor. 'It's quite tasty.'

'Sure,' I said, glancing around. Manny's shack was as spotless within as without.

'Pull up a chair.'

There were no chairs. I sat on the rug.

'I'm Ernst, by the way,' said the dog, offering me his paw.

'Jack Sperry,' I said, shaking limb extremities with Ernst. 'You talk,' I observed.

'A bioelectronic implant, modifying my larynx.'

Manny sidled into the kitchenette. Lifting a copper kettle from his kerosene stove, he filled a pair of earthenware mugs with boiling water then added heaping spoonfuls of Donaldson's Drinkable Coffee crystals.

'You said fresh,' I noted with Veritasian candour.

'It's fresh to *us*,' said the Pope.

'Want to hear a talking dog joke?' Ernst inquired.

'No,' I replied, truthfully.

'Oh,' said the dog, evidently wounded by my frankness.

Manny returned from the kitchenette with a Coca-Cola tray bearing the coffee mugs plus a cream pitcher and a canister marked *Salt*.

'It's a sterile world up there. Sterile, stifling, spiritually depleting.' Manny set the tray beside me and rolled his eyes heavenward. 'And before long it will all be ours. You doubt me? Listen – already we've placed twenty dissemblers in the legislature. A person with our talents has no trouble getting elected.'

'You mean – you're going to conquer Veritas?' I asked, making a point of not looking Manny in the eye.

The Pope slammed his palms against his ears. '*Please.*'

'Don't say "conquer",' admonished the dog.

'We're going to *reform* Veritas,' said Manny.

I stared at the rug. 'Truth is beauty, your Holiness.' Splaying my fingers, I ticked off a familiar litany. 'In the Age of Lies, politicians misled, advertisers overstated, clerics exaggerated—'

'Satirev's founders had nothing against telling the truth.'

Manny tapped his yarmulke. 'But they hated their inability to do otherwise. Honesty without choice, they said, is slavery with a smile.' He pointed toward the ceiling with his coffee mug. 'Truth above . . . ' He set his mug on the floor. 'Dignity below.' He chuckled softly. 'In Satirev, we opt for the latter. Do you like it sweet?'

'Huh?'

'Your coffee. Sweet?'

'I *would* like some sugar, matter of fact.'

The Pope handed me the salt canister. I shook some grains into my palm and licked. It was sugar.

'My heart is broken,' said Manny, laying a hand on his chest. 'I feel absolutely devastated about your Toby.'

'You do?'

'I'm crushed.'

'You don't even know him.'

'What you're doing is so *noble*.'

'I think so too,' said Ernst. 'And I'm only a dog.'

Manny shook Satirevian salt into his coffee. 'I have just one question. Listen carefully. Do you love your son?'

'That would depend on—'

'I don't mean love him, I mean *love* him. Crazy, unconditional, non-Veritasian love.'

Surprisingly – to myself if not the Pope – I didn't have to think about my answer. 'I love him,' I asserted, looking Manny in the eye. 'Crazy, unconditional, non-Veritasian . . .'

'Then you're in,' said Manny.

'Congratulations,' said the dog.

'I must warn you – the treatment doesn't take in all cases.' Manny sipped his Donaldson's. 'I advise you to throw everything you've got into it, your very soul, even if you're convinced you don't have one. Please don't look me in the eye.'

I turned away, uncertain whether to rejoice at being admitted or to brood over the possibility of failure. 'What are my chances, would you say?'

'First-rate,' said Manny.

'Truly excellent,' Ernst agreed.

'I'd bet money on it,' the Pope elaborated.

59

'Of course,' said the dog, 'we could be lying.'

On Sunday morning Martina and I hiked through the flurry of five-leaf clovers outside the Centre for Creative Wellness and, reaching the top of the hill, placed a call to Arnold Cook at his home in Locke Borough. After claiming to be my wife, Martina told him I'd been diagnosed with double pneumonia and wouldn't be coming to work for at least a week. Her fabulation gave me a terrible headache and also, truth to tell, a kind of sexual thrill.

The chief curator offered his qualified sympathy, and that was that. What a marvellous tool, lying, I thought: so practical and uncomplicated. I was beginning to understand its pervasive popularity in days gone by.

Together Martina and I strolled through the park, Franz Beauchamp hovering blatantly in the background. She grasped my right hand; my fingers became five erogenous zones. Today she would return to Veritas, she explained, where she'd finally lined up a job writing campaign speeches for Doreen Hutter, a Descartes Borough representative.

'I'll miss you,' I said.

'I'll be back,' she said, massaging her baroque braid with her free hand. 'Like all dissemblers, I'm obliged to immerse myself in Satirev ninety days a year. I'll be spending next Friday on the Jordan, fishing for ferrets.'

'Will you visit me?' I asked this zaftig and exotic woman.

She stared into the sky and nodded. 'With luck you'll be a liar by then,' she said, tracking a pig with her decorous eyes. 'If you have any words of truth for me, you'd better spill them now.'

'Truth?'

'We dissemblers can handle it, every now and then.'

'Well, I suppose I'd have to say . . . ' The reality of my condition dawned on me even as I spoke it. 'I'd have to say I'm a little bit in love with you, Martina.'

'Only a little bit?' she asked, leading me to the riverbank, Franz at our heels.

'These things are hard to quantify.' Two gondolas were lashed to the dock, riding the wake of a passing outboard motorboat. 'May I ask how you feel about me?'

'I'd prefer not to say.' Martina splayed her fingers, working free of my grasp. 'Ultimately there'd be nothing in it for either of us, nothing but grief.' She climbed into her gondola and, assuming the pilot's position in the stern, lowered her oar. 'I'm certain you'll become a Satirevian,' she said, casting off. 'I have great faith in you, Jack,' she called as she vanished into the three-thousand-watt sunrise.

The current carried Franz and me south, past a succession of riverfront cottages encrusted with casuistry: welcome mats, flower boxes, plaster lawn ornaments in the forms of Cupids and little Dutch girls. My guardian landed the gondola before a two-storey clapboard building painted a bright pink and surmounted by the words HOTEL PARADISE in flashing neon. A stone wall hemmed the grounds, broken by a massive gateway in which was suspended an iron portcullis, also painted pink. Bars of pink iron crisscrossed the hotel windows like strokes of a censor's pen.

A sudden *skreee*: the portcullis, ascending with the grinding gracelessness of an automated garage door. Franz led me beneath the archway, up a pink cement path, and through the central portal to the front desk. He gave my name to the clerk – *Leopold*, according to his badge – a horse-faced, overweight, fortyish man dressed in a Hawaiian shirt so loud it invited legislation. After confirming that they were indeed expecting a Jack Sperry from Plato Borough, Leopold issued me a pink tunic with NOVITIATE stamped on the chest. It was as baggy as a gown from the Centre for Creative Wellness, and I had no trouble slipping it on over my street clothes.

'You look real spiffy in that,' said Leopold.

'You're one of the homeliest people I've ever met,' I felt bound to inform him.

The chief bellhop, a spidery old man whose skin resembled a cantaloupe rind, guided me down a long hallway decorated with Giotto and Rembrandt reproductions, Franz following as always, my eternal shadow. We paused before a pink, rivetted door that seemed more likely to lead to a bank vault than a hotel room – it even had a combination lock. 'Your suite,' the bellhop said as the three of us stepped inside.

Suite. Sure. It was smaller than the Holy See, and sparser: no rugs, no chairs, no windows. The walls were clean and predictably pink. Two male novitiates, one tall, one short, rested on adjacent cots, smoking cigarettes. 'Your roommates,' said the bellhop as he and Franz exited. The door thudded shut, then came the muffled clicks of the tumblers being randomized.

'I'm William,' said my tall roommate; he could have been a power forward with the Plato Borough Competents. 'William Bell.'

'Ira Temple,' said his scrawny companion.

'Jack Sperry,' I said.

We spent the next hour swapping life stories.

Ira, I learned, was a typical dissembler-in-training. He hated Veritas. He had to get out. Anything, he argued, even dishonesty, was superior to what he called his native city's confusion of the empirical with the true.

William's story was closer to my own. His older sister Charlotte, the one person on Earth who mattered to him, had recently landed on Amaranth, a planet that existed only in her mind. By learning to lie, William reasoned, he might travel to Charlotte's mythic world and either release her from its mad gravity or take up residence there himself.

The door swung open and in came a small, dusky, stoop-shouldered man with a bald head and a style of walking that put me in mind of a duck with osteoporosis. 'During the upcoming week, you're all going to fall in love with me,' he said abruptly, waving his clipboard. 'I'm going to treat you so well, you'll think you've died and gone to heaven.' He issued a wicked little wink. 'That's a lie. I'm Gregory Harness, Manny Ginsburg's liaison. You may call me Lucky,' he said with an insistent, rapid-fire bonhomie. 'The Pope deeply regrets not being here to orient you personally, but his busy schedule did not permit . . . anyhow, you get the drift of his bullshit. Which one of you's Sperry?'

I raised my hand.

'I heard about your sick child,' said Lucky. 'Heartrending. Tragic. Believe me, Sperry, I'll be rooting for you all the way.'

And so it was upon us, our absorption in lies, our descent into deception, our headlong, brainfirst plunge into Satirevian reality.

At the crack of dawn Lucky herded us into his pick-up truck and took us to a place where money grew on trees, a pecuniary orchard so vast it could have paid the interest on Veritas's national debt. We spent a sweaty, gruelling day under the celestial lamps, harvesting basket after basket of five-dollar bills.

On Tuesday morning the weather engineers contrived a fearsome blizzard, squall upon squall of molten snow bringing Satirev to a total standstill and inspiring Lucky to issue us broad-scooped shovels. 'Clean it up,' he demanded, 'every highway, street, alley, path, sidewalk and wharf.' And so we did, our skin erupting in second-degree burns as we carried heap after heap of steaming precipitate to the Jordan and dropped them over the banks. Lucky mopped our brows with towels dipped in ice water, slaked our thirst with lemonade, soothed our blistered backs with eucalyptus oil – but he kept us on the job all day.

Wednesday: a tedious morning of shoeing six-legged horses, a wearying afternoon of decorating Satirev's innumerable rock gardens. My companions and I felt that, for stones, these creatures were extraordinarily loquacious and singularly self-pitying. The stones lamented their lack of mobility and prestige. They said it was hell being a stone. Cut them, they claimed, and they would bleed.

Further lies, Thursday's lies – our task master loaded his truck with cans of spray paint and shunted us across Satirev, stopping at every public park along the way and ordering us to turn the grass purple, the roses blue and the violets red, an ordeal that left my co-apprentices and me so speckled we looked like amalgams of all the Jackson Pollocks I'd ever criticized. That night, as I lay on my cot in the Paradise, my stunned brain swirled with deceptions – with lavender cabbages and crimson potatoes, with indigo jungles and chartreuse icebergs, with square baseballs, skinny whales, tall dwarves and snakes with long, pale, supple legs.

More lies – lies, lies, lies. On Friday, Lucky gave us ·22-calibre hunting rifles, instructed us in their use and, exploiting the handicap of our Veritasian upbringings, made us swear we wouldn't use them to escape. 'Before the day is out, you must each bring down a flying pig. Don't let the low comedy of their anatomy fool you – they're smarter than they look.' Thus did I find myself crouched behind a forest of cat-o'-nine-tails on the banks of the Jordan, my ·22 poised on my knees, my mind turning over the manifest rationale behind my deconditioning. A black, bulbous shape glided across the river, like the shadow that might be cast by a gigantic horsefly, and I recalled the perusal I'd made of *Alice in Wonderland* before criticizing it. 'The time has come,' the Walrus said, 'to talk of many things.' I grabbed the rifle, took aim; the shape flew along the equator of my telescopic sight, eastward to the axis. 'Of shoes – and ships – and sealing wax – of cabbages and kings.' I fired. 'And why the sea is boiling hot.' The bewildered animal fell squealing. 'And whether pigs have wings.' My bleeding prey hit the water.

When your every muscle aches with the effects of a currency harvest, you do not doubt that money grows on trees. When your entire epidermis is branded with the aftermath of two hundred-degree snowflakes, you cannot but accept their existence. When every particle of your concentration is fixed upon blasting a winged pig out of the sky, you do not question its species's ontological status.

The Hotel Paradise had but one eatery, an immaculate malt shop called the Russian Tea Room, and on Friday night Lucky took us there for dinner. Glistery white tiles covered the walls. The stools – red vinyl cushions poised on glistening steel stalks – resembled Art Deco mushrooms. The menu bulged with murdered cows, euphemistically named 'cheese steaks', 'hot dogs', 'hamburgers', and 'beef tacos'. Lucky told us to order whatever we liked.

'I've been driving you all pretty hard,' he confessed after our meals arrived.

64

'An understatement,' I replied.

Lucky twisted the cap off a bottle of Quasitomato Ketchup from Veritas. 'Tell me, men, do you feel any different?'

'Different?' said Ira Temple, voraciously consuming a 'beef taco'. 'Not really.'

William Bell bit into his 'cheeseburger'. 'I'm the same man I always was.'

'Saturday's schedule is pretty intense,' said Lucky, shaking blobs of ketchup onto his French fries. 'You'll be digging sugar out of the salt mines, attending a linguistics seminar with some golden retrievers, carrying steer haunches over to the Pope for him to bless. In my experience, though, if you're not a liar by now, you never will be.' With a directness rarely found in Satirev, Lucky looked William in the eye. 'What do pigs have, son?'

'Huh?'

'Pigs. What do they have? You've been dealing with pigs lately – you know about them.'

William stared at his half-eaten cow. He pondered the question for nearly a minute. At last he raised his head, closed his eyes tightly and let out the sort of delighted yelp an Age-of-Lies child might have issued on Christmas morning. 'Pigs have w-wings!'

'What did you say?'

'W-w-wings!' William leaped from his chair and danced around the table. 'Wings!' he sang. 'Wings! Pigs have wings!'

'Good job, William!' Ira shouted, his face betraying a mixture of envy and anxiety.

Lucky smiled, ate a fry and thrust his fork toward Ira. 'Now – you. Tell me about money, Ira. Where does money grow?'

Ira took a deep breath. 'Well, that's not an easy question. Some people would say it doesn't *grow* at all. Others might argue . . .'

'Money, son. Where does money grow?'

'On trees!' Ira suddenly screamed.

'On *what*?'

'Money grows on trees!'

'And I'm the Queen of Sheba!' said William.

'I'm the King of France!' said Ira.

'I can fly!' said William.

'I can walk on water!' said Ira.

'God protects the innocent!'

'The guilty never go free!'

'Love is eternal!'

'Life is too!'

Lucky laid his knobbly hand on my shoulder. 'What's the deal with snow, Jack?' he asked. 'What is snow like?'

The appropriate word formed in my brain. I could sense it riding the tip of my tongue like a grain of sand. 'It's . . . it's . . .'

'Is it hot, for example?' asked Lucky.

'Snow is h-h-h—'

'Hot?'

'Cold!' I shrieked. 'Snow is cold,' I moaned.

William shot me an agonized glance. 'Jack, you've got it all wrong.'

'Don't you remember that blizzard?' asked Ira.

I quivered with nausea, reeled with defeat. Damn. Shit. 'The stuff they make here is a *fraud*.' Jack Sperry versus Xavier's Plague – and now the disease would win. 'It's not snow at all.'

'Snow is hot,' said Ira.

'It's *cold!*' Rising from my chair, I stumbled blindly around the Russian Tea Room. 'Pigs don't fly! Dogs don't talk! Truth is beauty!'

I left.

The hotel lobby was dark and pungent, suffused with the Jordan's sugary aroma. The night clerk slept at his post. Franz Beauchamp sat in a wicker chair beside a potted palm, his long face shadowed by a Panama hat.

I staggered to the front door. It was locked. But of course: one left Satirev filled with either lies or scopolamine, illusion or amnesia; there was no third path.

'Treatment isn't taking, huh?' said Franz as he approached. 'Don't be discouraged.'

'I'm beaten,' I groaned.

'Now, now – you still have tomorrow.' Franz removed

66

his Panama, placing it over his heart – a gesture of grief, I decided, anticipatory mourning for Toby Sperry. 'Someone wants to see you,' he said.

'Huh?'

'You have a visitor.'

'Who?'

'This way.'

He led me past the sleeping clerk and down the east corridor to a steel door uncharacteristically free of catches, bolts and locks. The sign said, VIDEO GAMES. Franz turned the handle.

There were no video games in the Video Games Room.

There was a blood-red billiard table.

A print of Picasso's *The Young Women of Avignon.*

Martina Coventry.

'Hi, critic. We had a date, remember?'

'To tell you the truth, I'd forgotten.'

' "To tell you the truth"? What kind of talk is that for a Satirevian?' Martina came toward me, her extended hand fluttering like a wondrous bird. 'You look unhappy, dear.'

'I'm no Satirevian.' I reached out and captured her plump fingers. 'Never will be.'

Martina tapped the brim of Franz's Panama. 'Mr Sperry and I require privacy,' she told him. 'Don't worry, we're not going to have sex or anything.'

Though convulsed with misery and self-loathing, I nevertheless noticed how Martina was dressed. If employed as a lampshade, her miniskirt wouldn't have reached the socket. The strap of her madras bag lay along her cleavage, pulling her LIFE IS A BANQUET T-shirt tight against her body and making her breasts seem like two adjacent spinnakers puffed full of wind.

Franz tipped his hat and ducked out of the room.

'Let's get your mind off your deconditioning.' Martina hopped on to the table and stretched out. She looked like a relief map of some particularly lewd and mountainous nation. 'Lie down next to me.'

'Not a good idea,' I said. True: a roll on the felt wasn't going to solve my problems. I should be pumping Martina's mind and no other part of her; I should be trying to learn how she herself had managed the crucial transition from Veritasian to liar.

She said, 'You don't want to?'

I gulped loudly. 'No, I don't.' My blood lurched toward the temperature of Satirevian snow.

'No?'

'I'm *married*, remember? I don't want to have sex with you.'

I did, of course. In my heart of hearts, I did – and now came the correlative of my desire, drawing both Martina's attention and my own.

I don't want to have sex with you, I'd said.

Yet here was the resolute little hero, shaping the crotch of my overalls into a denim sculpture.

So I'd lied! For the first time since my brainburn, I'd lied!

I pulled off my tunic, slipped out of my overalls. ' "I hide my wings inside my soul",' I quoted, climbing atop Martina.

Deftly she removed my undershorts; my erection broke free, a priapic jailbreak. I'd done it, by damn. I might have a Veritasian penis, but I'd finally acquired a Satirevian tongue.

' "Their feathers soft and dry"!' I cried, shucking off Martina's skirt.

' "And when the world's not looking"!' she whooped.

' "I take them out and fly"!'

I had to apply the brakes on my Adequate almost a dozen times as I descended the southern face of Mount Prosaic and headed into the lush green valley below. Cabin after cabin, hut after hut, Camp Ditch-the-Kids was strung along a strip of pine barren midway between the swiftly flowing Wishywashy and a placid oxbow lake. For the first time, it occurred to me that Toby might not like the idea of leaving two days early. With its fearsome dedication to frivolity, its endless amusements and diversions, Ditch-the-Kids was the sort of place a seven-year-old could easily imagine living in forever.

As I pulled up behind the administration building, a gang of pre-adolescent children in yellow Ditch-the-Kids T-shirts marched by, clutching fishing rods. I studied their faces. No Toby. Snatches of the counsellor's pep talk drifted toward me, something to the effect that acid rain was sterilizing Lake Commonplace so it really didn't matter how much they caught, the fish were all doomed anyway.

I entered the building, a slapdash pile of tar paper and cedar shingles. A grizzled man with a three-day beard sat behind the desk, reading the August issue of *Beatoff*.

'I'm Toby Sperry's father,' I said. 'And you're . . . ?'

'Ralph Kitto.' The camp director eyed me suspiciously. 'Look, Mr Sperry, there's no question we were pretty irresponsible, leaving that rat trap out in the open as we did, but I don't believe you have a criminal case against us.'

'It's not my intention to sue you,' I told him, savouring the spectacle of joy and relief blossoming on his face. Little did he know I could have been lying.

'Will Toby be okay? I've been feeling a certain amount of guilt about this matter. Nothing I can't handle, but—'

'I'm here to bring him home,' I said. 'He's going into the hospital tomorrow.'

'Life is a tough business, isn't it?' Ralph Kitto fanned himself with *Beatoff*. 'Take me, for example. Sure wish I could find a better line of work.'

'I imagine these kids drive you crazy — figuratively crazy.'

'Vodka helps. I get drunk frequently.'

Kitto consulted his master schedule and told me Toby was probably still on the archery field, a half-mile south down the Wishywashy. I paid the balance due on my son's tuition, thanked the director for his willingness to take on such an unrewarding job, and set out along the river.

When I reached the field, my son had just missed the bull's-eye by less than an inch.

'Nice shooting, Toby, old buddy!'

He maintained his bowman's stance, transfixed not only by the fact of my arrival but also, no doubt, by the content of my greeting. 'Dad, what are *you* doing here?'

I hadn't seen him in a month. He seemed taller, leaner, swarthier — older — standing there in his grimy yellow T-shirt and the blue jeans he'd shredded into shorts last spring.

'I've come for you,' I told him, moving as close as I could without making it obvious I was scanning him for symptoms. His hair was as thick, dark and healthy-looking as ever. His eyes sparkled, his frame looked firm, his tanned skin held no trace of blue.

'No, I'm taking the bus Sunday.' He nocked an arrow. 'Mom's picking me up.'

'The plan's been changed. She had to go out of town – there's a big UFO story breaking in the Hegelian Desert.' I experienced a small but irrefutable pleasure, the sweet taste of truth bending in my mouth. 'We'd better get your stuff packed. Where's your cabin?'

Toby unnocked the arrow and used it to indicate a cluster of yurts about twenty yards from the targets.

The archery instructor approached, a woodsy, weathered fellow with a mild limp. Toby introduced me as the best father a boy'd ever had. He said he loved me. So strange, I thought, the spontaneous little notions that run through the heads of pre-burn children.

My son turned in his bow, and we started toward his cupcake-shaped cabin.

'You've got a nice tan, Toby. You look real healthy. Gosh, it's good to see you.'

'Dad, you're talking so *funny*.'

'I'll bet you *feel* healthy too.'

'Lately I've been getting headaches.'

I gritted my teeth. 'I'm sure that's nothing to worry about.'

'Wish I wasn't leaving so soon,' he said as we climbed the crooked wooden steps to his room. 'Barry Maxwell and I were supposed to hunt snakes tomorrow.'

'Listen, Toby, this is a better deal than you think. You're going to get an entire second vacation.' The space was only slightly more chaotic than I'd anticipated – clothes in ragged heaps, *Encyclopedia Britannica* comics in amorphous piles. 'We're going to live in a magic kingdom under the ground. Just you and me.'

'What sort of magic kingdom?' he asked sceptically.

'Oh, you'll love it, Toby. We'll go fishing and eat ice cream.'

Toby smiled hugely, brightly – a Satirevian smile. 'That

sounds neat.' He opened his footlocker and started cramming it full: crafts projects, T-shirts, dungarees, poncho, comics, flashlight, canteen, mess kit. 'Will Mom be coming?'

'No.'

'She'll miss all the fun.'

'She'll miss all the fun,' I agreed.

My son held up a hideous and lopsided battleship, proudly announcing that he'd made it in woodworking class. 'How do you like it, Dad?'

'Why, Toby,' I told him, 'it's absolutely beautiful.'

6

Twelve gates lead to the City of Lies. Every year, as his commitment to mendacity becomes increasingly clear, his dishonesty more manifestly reliable, the Satirevian convert is told the secret location of yet another entrance. Mere novitiates like myself knew only one: the storm drainage tunnel near the corner of Third and Bruno in Nietzsche Borough.

So many ways to descend, I thought as Toby and I negotiated the dank, mossy labyrinth beneath Veritas. Ladders, sloping sewer pipes, narrow stone stairways – we used them all, our flashlights cutting through the darkness like machetes clearing away underbrush. My son loved every minute of it. 'Wow!' he exclaimed whenever some disgusting wonder appeared – a slug the size of a banana, a subterranean lake filled with frogs, a spider's web as large and sturdy as a trampoline. 'Neat!'

Reaching our destination, we settled into the Hotel Paradise. Unlike my previous accommodations, our assigned suite was sunny and spacious, with glass doors opening onto a wrought-iron balcony from which one could readily glimpse the local fauna. 'Dad, the horses around here have six legs!' Toby hopped up and down with excitement. 'The rats chase the cats! The pigs have wings! This really *is* a magic kingdom!'

It soon became obvious that the whole of Satirev had been anticipating our arrival. We were the men of the hour. The Paradise guards immediately learned our faces, letting us come and go as we pleased. Franz and Lucky gushed over Toby as if he were a long-lost brother. Whenever we strolled around the community, total strangers would come up to us and, confirming our identities, give Satirev's tragic child a candy bar or a small toy, his father a hug of encouragement and affirmation.

Even Felicia Krakower was prepared. After drawing a

sample of Toby's blood – we told him the kingdom had to make certain the tourists weren't carrying germs – she retired to her office and came back holding a stuffed animal, an astonishingly comical baboon with acrobatic eyes and a squarish, doglike snout.

'This is for you, Rainbow Boy,' she said.

Toby's face grew knotted and tense; he gulped audibly. He was not too old for stuffed animals, merely too old to enjoy them without shame.

'He needs a name, don't you think?' said Dr Krakower. 'Not a silly name, I'd say. Something dignified.'

I performed my survey, the one I took every hour. The facts were becoming irrefutable – the bluish cast of his skin, the thinness of his hair.

Toby relaxed, smiled. 'Dignified,' he said. 'Not silly. Oh, yes.' Clearly, he'd sensed the truth of his new home: in Satirev everything was permitted; in Satirev no boy grew up before his time. 'His name is Barnaby. Barnaby Baboon.' Frowning, Toby rammed the tip of his tongue into the corner of his mouth. 'I think he might be carrying some germs.'

'Rainbow Boy, you're absolutely right.' Dr Krakower pried a wad of cotton batting out of Barnaby's arm with her syringe. 'We'd better take a stuffing sample.'

That night, the minute my son fell asleep, I ran to the phone booth outside the Paradise and called the Centre for Creative Wellness. Krakower told me exactly what I expected to hear: the Xavier's test was positive.

'There's still plenty of hope,' she insisted.

'I know what you mean,' I said, shivering in the hot summer darkness. Positive. *Positive.* 'If we give Toby the right outlook, his immune system will kick in and *bang* – remission.'

'Exactly.'

'How many years might a remission last?'

'You can't tell about remissions, Jack. Some of them last a long, long time.'

I placed a call to Veritas.

'Hi, Helen.'

'Jack? *Now* you call? *Now*, after ten whole days?'

'I've been busy.'

'Your curator sent a get-well card. Are you sick?'

'I'm feeling better.'

'This is a bad time to talk,' she said. 'I'm due at the bus station.'

'No, you're not. I picked up Toby on Sunday.'

'You *what?*'

'He's got to be with *me* now. I can give him the right outlook.'

'You mean – you're one of them?'

'Dogs can talk, Helen.'

I pictured her turning white, cringing. 'Shut up!' she screamed. 'I want my son back! Bring me my son, you tropological shithead!'

'I *love* him.'

'Bring him back!'

'I can cure him.'

'Jack!'

As the hot, soggy July melded into a hotter, soggier August, my son and I began spending long hours in the outdoors – or, rather, in those open spaces that in Satirev functioned as the outdoors. Together we explored the community's swampy frontiers, collecting bugs and amphibians for Toby's scale-model zoo. The money orchards, meanwhile, proved excellent for archery – we would nock our arrows and aim at the five-dollar bills – while the broiling snowfields soon became littered with the results of our sculpting efforts: snowmen, snowdogs, snowcows, snowbaboons. It was all a matter of having a good pair of insulated gloves.

Finally there was the Jordan, perfect for swimming and, when we could borrow a gondola, fishing. 'Do you like this place?' I asked Toby as I threaded my line with a double-barbed hook.

'It's pretty weird.' Furiously he worked his reel, hauling an aquatic armadillo on board.

'You're having a terrific time, though, aren't you, buddy? You're feeling cheerful.'

'Oh, yeah,' he said evenly.

'What do you like? Do you like making snowmen?'

'The snowmen are great.'

'And the fishing?'

'I like the fishing.' Placing his boot on the armadillo's left gill, Toby yanked the hook out of its mouth.

'And you like our archery tournaments too, don't you?' I marvelled at the armadillo's design – its lozenge-shaped body, sleek scales, dynamic fins. 'And the swimming?'

'Uh-huh. I wish Mom were here.'

I baited my own hook with a Satirevian snail. 'So do I. What else do you like?'

'I don't know.' In a spasmodic act of mercy, he tossed the armadillo overboard. 'I like the way strangers give me candy.'

'And you like the fishing too, right?'

'I already said that,' Toby replied patiently. 'Dad, why is my hair falling out?'

'W-what?'

'My hair. And my skin looks funny too.'

I shuddered, pricking my thumb with the fishhook. 'Buddy, there's something we should talk about. Remember that blood sample Dr Krakower took? It seems you've got a few germs in you. Nothing serious – Xavier's Plague, it's called.'

'Whose plague?'

'Xavier's.'

'Then how come *I* got it?'

'Lots of people get it.'

Toby impaled a snail on his fishhook. 'Is that why my hair . . . ?'

'Probably. They might have to give you some medicine. You're not really sick.' God, how I loved being able to say that. Such power. 'The thing is to stay cheerful. Just say to yourself, "Those bad old Xavier's germs can't hurt *me*. My immune system's too strong." '

'My what?'

'Immune system. Say it, Toby. Say, "Those bad old Xavier's germs can't hurt *me*." Go ahead.'

' "Those bad old Xavier's germs can't hurt *me*",' he repeated haltingly. 'Is that true, Dad?'

'You bet. You aren't worried, are you?'

Toby rubbed his blue forehead. 'I guess not.'

'That's my buddy.'

If my son wasn't too old for stuffed animals, then he wasn't too old for bedtime stories. We read together every night, snuggling amid the Paradise's soft buttery sheets and smooth cotton blankets, working our way through a stack of volumes that had somehow escaped the Wittgenstein's predations – *Tom Sawyer, Treasure Island, Corbeau the Pirate* and, best of all, a leatherbound, gilt-edged collection of fairy tales. Perusing the Brothers Grimm, I trembled not only with the thrill of forbidden fruit – how daring I felt, acting out material I'd normally be reading only in prelude to burning it – but with the odd amoralities and psychosexual insights of the stories themselves. Toby's favourite was 'Rumpelstiltskin', with its unexpected theme of an old man's hunger for a baby. My own preference was 'Sleeping Beauty'. I roundly identified with the father – with his mad, Herodlike campaign to circumvent his daughter's destiny by destroying every spinning wheel in the kingdom. I thought him heroic.

'Why did Rumpelstiltskin want a baby?' Toby asked.

'A baby is the best thing there is,' I replied. I felt I was telling the truth. 'Rumpelstiltskin knew what he needed.'

Whenever Martina was in Satirev, she joined our expeditions – hiking, swimming, fishing, bug collecting – and I couldn't quite decide what Toby made of her. They got along famously, even to the point of scatalogical private jokes involving Barnaby Baboon, but occasionally I caught a glimmer of unease in my son's eyes. Were he a post-burn kid, of course, he would have been frank. Dad, is Martina your mistress? Dad, do you and Martina have sex?

To which the truthful answer would have been: no. Since Toby's arrival, I had lost my urge for erotic adventures. Martina did not protest; like me, she rather regretted our romp on the billiard table: adultery was wrong, after all – even a dissembler knew that. Thus had Martina and I entered that vast population of men and women whose friendship has crossed the copulation barrier but once, followed by retrenchment and retreat, an entire affair compacted into one memorable screw.

Most nights, the three of us went to dinner in the Russian Tea Room. The staff doted on Toby; he got all the hamburgers he could eat, all the hot dogs, all the French fries, all the milkshakes. Nobody could say the Tea Room wasn't doing its part to keep Toby cheerful, nobody could say it wasn't putting him in a salubrious mood. The manager was a thin, wiry, exuberant man in his early fifties named Norbert Vore (evidently he did not partake of his own fattening and enervating menu), and upon sensing that from the boy's viewpoint the restaurant was deficient in desserts, he immediately read up on the matter, soon learning how to prepare transcendent strawberry shortcake and ambrosial lemon-meringue pie. Norbert's baked Alaska, fudge brownies, and bing-cherry tarts kept Toby grinning ear to ear. His chocolate parfaits were so lush and uplifting they seemed in themselves a cure.

It was in the Russian Tea Room that Toby and I first noted a curious fashion among Satirevians. About a quarter of them wore sweatshirts emblazoned with a Valentine-style heart poised above the initials H.E.A.R.T. 'HEART, what's that?' my son asked Martina one evening as we were ploughing through a particularly outrageous ice cream treat – a concoction Norbert had dubbed 'A Month of Sundaes'.

'It's a kind of club – the members get together and talk about philosophy. You know what philosophy is, Toby?'

'No.'

'The *H* stands for Happiness, the *E* for Equals.'

'And the *A*, *R* and *T*?' asked Toby.

'Art, Reason and Truth.'

H.E.A.R.T. It was, Martina explained after Toby went to bed, an organization the year-rounders had formed for the sake of, as she put it, 'thinking good thoughts about your son and thereby hastening his cure'. HEART, the Healing and Ecstasy Association for the Recovery of Toby. They met every Tuesday evening. They were planning to start a newsletter.

I had never been so profoundly moved, so totally touched, in my life. My soul sang, my throat got hard as a crab apple. 'Martina, that's *terrific*. Why didn't you tell me about HEART?'

'Because it gives me the creeps, that's why.'

'The creeps?'

'Your son is sick, Jack. *Sick*. He's going to need more than HEART. He's going to need . . . well, a miracle.'

'HEART *is* a miracle, Martina. Don't you get it? It *is* a miracle.'

There is nothing quite so exhilarating as spending large amounts of time with your child, and nothing quite so tedious. I'll be honest: when Martina offered to relieve me of Toby for an hour or two – she wanted to help him find specimens for his miniature zoo – I told her to take all day. Even Sleeping Beauty's father, I'm sure, grew bored with her on occasion.

It was an hour past his bedtime when Toby returned to the Paradise, laden with the day's haul – a dozen bottles and cages filled with rubbery newts, glutinous salamanders, spiky centipedes, and disgruntled tree frogs whose cries sounded like bicycle bells.

He could not enjoy them.

'Dad, I don't feel so good,' he said, setting the various terrariums on the coffee table.

'Oh?' So here it comes, I thought. Now it begins. 'What do you mean?'

'My head hurts.' Toby clutched his belly. 'And my stomach. Is it those germs, Dad?'

'Just remember, in the long run they can't hurt you.'

''Cause of my immune system?'

'Smart boy.'

Toby woke up repeatedly that night, his temperature lurching toward 103, flesh trembling, bones rattling, teeth chattering. He sweated like a bill-picker labouring in the money orchards. I had to change the sheets four times. They stank of brine.

'I think we'd better drop by the hospital tomorrow,' I told him.

'Hospital? I thought I wasn't really sick.'

'You *aren't* really sick.' Oh, the power, the power. 'Dr Krakower wants to give you some medicine, that's all.'

'I don't think I can sleep, Dad. Will you read to me about Rumpelstiltskin or pirates or something?'

'Of course. Sure. Just stay happy, and you'll be fine.'

The next morning, I took Toby to the Centre for Creative Wellness, where he was assigned a place in the children's ward, a large private room that despite its spaciousness quickly seemed to fill with my son's disease, a sickly, sallow aura radiating from the bedframe, covering the nightstand, smothering the sway-backed parent's cot in the far corner. His skin got bluer; his temperature climbed: 103, 104, 104.5, 105, 105.5. By nightfall the lymph nodes under his arm had grown to resemble clusters of ossified grapes.

'We can get the fever down with acetaminophen and alcohol baths,' said Dr Krakower as she guided me into her office. 'And I think we should put him on pentamidine. It's been known to work wonders against *Pneumocystis carinii*.'

'Genuine wonders?'

'Oh, yes. We'd better set him up for intravenous feeding. I want to try pure oxygen too, maybe an inhalator. It'll keep his mind clear.'

'Doctor, if there's no remission . . .'

'We shouldn't talk like that.'

'If there's no remission, how long will he live?'

'Don't know.'

'Two weeks?'

'Oh, yes, two weeks for sure, Jack. I can practically *promise* you two weeks.'

Although Martina's speech-writing job for Borough Representative Doreen Hutter consumed all her mornings, she arranged to spend each afternoon at Toby's bedside, infusing him with happy thoughts. She invited him to imagine he was gradually entering a state of suspended animation, so that he could become the first boy ever sent beyond our solar system in a spaceship: hence the inhalator squeezing and expanding his chest, conditioning his lungs for interstellar travel; hence the plastic tube flowing into his left arm, giving him enough food for a year in hibernation;

hence the plastic mask – the 'rocket jockey's oxygen supply' – strapped over his mouth and nose.

'When you wake up, Toby, you'll be on another planet – the magical world of Lulaloon!'

'Lulaloon?' The oxygen mask made him sound distant, as if he were already in space. 'Is it as good as Satirev?'

'Better.'

'As good as summer camp?'

'Twice as good.'

Toby stretched out, putting a crimp in his glucose tube, stopping the flow of what Martina had told him were liquid French fries. 'I like your games,' he said.

I stroked my son's balding scalp. 'How's your imagination working?' I asked him.

'Pretty good, I guess.'

'Can you picture Mr Medicine zapping those nasty old Xavier's germs?'

'Sure.'

' "Zap 'em, Mr Medicine. Zap 'em dead!" Right, Toby?'

'Right,' he wheezed.

For over a week, Toby remained appropriately chipper, but then a strange Veritasian scepticism crept over him, darkening his spirits as relentlessly as the *Pneumocystis carinii* were darkening his lungs. 'I feel sick,' he told Dr Krakower one afternoon as she prepared to puncture him with a second IV needle, in the right arm this time. 'I don't think that medicine's any good. I'm cold.'

'Well, Rainbow Boy,' she said, 'Xavier's isn't any fun – I'll be the first to admit that – but you'll be up and running before you know it.'

'My head still hurts, and my—'

'When one medicine doesn't work,' I hastily inserted, 'there's always another we can try – right, Dr Krakower?'

'Oh, yes.'

Martina took Toby's hand, giving it a hard squeeze as Krakower slid the needle into his vein.

Toby winced and asked, 'Do children ever die?'

'That's a strange question, Rainbow Boy,' said Krakower. 'Do they?'

'It's very, very rare.' The doctor opened the stopcock on Toby's meperidine drip.

'She means never,' I explained. 'Don't even think about it, Toby. It's bad for your immune system.'

'He's really cold,' said Martina, her hand still clasped in Toby's. 'Can we turn up the heat?'

'It's up all the way,' said Krakower. 'His electric blanket's on full.'

The narcotic seeped into Toby's neurons. 'I'm cold,' he said woozily.

'You'll be warm soon,' I lied. 'Say, "Zap 'em, Mr Medicine. Zap 'em." '

'Zap 'em, Mr Medicine,' said Toby, fading. 'Zap . . . zap . . . zap . . .'

So it was time to get serious; it was time for Sleeping Beauty's father to track down every last spinning wheel and chop it to bits. The minute Krakower left, I turned to Martina and asked her to put me in touch with the president of the Healing and Ecstasy Association for the Recovery of Toby.

Instead of complying, Martina merely snorted. 'Jack, I can't help feeling you're riding for a fall.'

'What do you mean?'

'A fall, Jack.'

'Such pessimism. Don't you know that psychoneuro-immunology is one of the key sciences of our age?'

'Just *look* at him, for Christ's sake. Look at Toby. He's living on borrowed time. You know that, don't you?'

'No, I *don't* know that.' I cast her a killing glance. 'Even if the time *is* borrowed, Martina, that doesn't mean it won't be the best time a boy's ever had.'

She gave me the facts I needed. Anthony Raines, Suite 42, Hotel Paradise.

I marched up the hill outside the Centre for Creative Wellness and placed the call. HEART's president answered on the first ring.

'Jack Sperry?' he gasped after I identified myself. '*The* Jack Sperry? Really? Goodness, what a coincidence. We've been hoping to interview you for *The Toby Times*.'

'For the what?'

'Our first issue comes out tomorrow. We'll be running stories about the fun you and Toby are having down here, his favourite toys and sports, what analgesics and antibiotics he's taking – all the things our members want to hear about.'

The Toby Times. I found the idea simultaneously inspiring and distasteful. 'Mr Raines, my son just entered the hospital, and I was hoping—'

'I know – it's our lead story. A setback, sure, but no reason to give up hope. Listen, Jack – may I call you Jack? – we people of the HEART know you're on the right track. Once Toby tunes in the cosmic pulse, his energy field will reintegrate, and then he's home free.'

The more Anthony Raines spoke in his calm, mellow voice, the better I felt – and the sharper my image of him became: a tall, raffish, golden-haired bohemian with bright blue eyes and a drooping, slightly disreputable moustache. 'Mr Raines, I want you to mobilize your forces.'

'Call me Anthony. What's up?'

'Just this – for the next two weeks, Toby Sperry's going to be the happiest child on Earth.' No spinning wheel would escape my notice, ran my silent, solemn pledge. 'Don't worry about the cost,' I added. 'We'll put it on my MasterDebt card.'

I pictured Anthony Raines organizing his buddhalike features into a resolute smile. 'Mr Sperry, the HEART stands ready to help your cause in every way it can.'

The next evening, Santa Claus visited the Centre for Creative Wellness.

His red suit glowed like an ember. His white beard lay on his chest like a frozen waterfall.

'Who are *you*?' Toby asked, struggling to sit up amid the tangle of rubber. Every day he seemed to acquire yet another IV need: glucose, meperidine, saline, Ringer's lactate, the various tubes swirling around him like an external circulatory system. 'Do I know you?' With a bold flourish he pulled off his plastic mask, as if this bulbous saint's mere presence had somehow unclogged his lungs.

'Hi, there, fella,' said Santa, chuckling heartily: Sebastian, of course – Sebastian Arboria – the fat and affable dissembler who'd led the meeting in the roundhouse; I'd empowered Anthony Raines to hire him for twenty dollars an hour. 'Call me Santa Claus. Saint Nicholas, if you prefer. Know what, Toby? Christmas is coming. Ever heard of Christmas?'

'I think we studied that in school. Isn't it supposed to be silly?'

'Silly?' said Sebastian with mock horror. 'Christmas is the most wonderful thing there is. If I were a young lad, I'd feel absolutely *great* about Christmas. I'd be looking forward to it with every cell of my body. I'd be so full of happiness there wouldn't be any room left for Xavier's Plague.'

'Is Christmas a warm time?' Toby was wholly without hair now. He was bald as an egg.

'The night before Christmas, I fly around the world in my sleigh, visiting every boy and girl, leaving good things behind.'

'Will you visit *me*?'

'Of course I'll visit you. What do you want for Christmas, Toby?'

'You can have *anything*,' I said. 'Right, Santa?'

'Yep, anything,' said Sebastian.

'I want to see my mother,' said Toby.

Felicia Krakower shuddered. 'That's not exactly Santa's department.'

'I want to get warm.'

Sebastian said, 'What I *mean* is . . . like a toy. I'll bring you a toy.'

'Pick something special,' I insisted. 'Say, that Power Pony you've been asking about.'

'No, that's for my *birthday*,' Toby corrected me.

'Why don't you get it for Christmas?' Martina suggested.

Toby slipped his rocket jockey's oxygen supply back on. 'Well . . . okay, I guess I *would* like a Power Pony.' His words bounced off the smooth green plastic.

Sebastian said, 'A *Power Pony*, eh? Well, well – we'll see what we can do. Any particular *kind* of Power Pony?'

'The kind for a big kid.' Toby's inhalator thumped like

a car riding on flat tyres. 'Maybe I look short to you, lying here in bed, but I'm really seven. Can he be brown?'

'So – a brown Power Pony for a seven-year-old, eh? I think we can manage that, and maybe a couple of surprises too.'

Toby's delighted giggle reverberated inside his mask. 'How long do I have to wait?'

'Christmas will be here before you know it,' I told him. 'It's just a couple of days away, right, Santa?'

'Right.'

'Will I be better by then?' Toby asked.

'There's a good chance of it, Rainbow Boy,' said Krakower, twisting the stopcock on Toby's meperidine drip. He was getting the stuff almost continuously now, as if he had two hearts, one pumping blood, the other pumping narcotics. 'It's highly likely.'

Furtively I opened my wallet and drew out my MasterDebt card. 'For Anthony Raines,' I whispered, pushing the plastic rectangle toward Sebastian. 'Everything goes on this.'

Sebastian extended his palm like a Squad officer stopping traffic. 'Keep your card,' he said. 'The HEART's picking up the tab, including my fee.' He stood fully erect, the pillow shifting under his wide black belt, and backed out of the room. 'So long, Toby – Merry Christmas!'

'Merry Christmas,' said Toby, coughing. He threw off his mask and turned to me. 'Did you hear that, Dad? Santa's coming back. I'm so *excited*.' His plum-coloured skin was luminous. 'He's going to bring me a Power Pony, and some surprises too. I can't *wait* for him to come back – I just can't *wait*.'

Martina said, 'We have to talk.'

'About what?'

'I think you know.'

She escorted me into the first-floor visitation lounge, a kind of indoor jungle. Everywhere, exotic pink blossoms sat amid lush green fronds the size of elephant ears. Fake, all of it: each petal was porcelain, each leaf glass.

'Jack, what you're doing simply isn't right.'

85

'In your opinion, Martina.' I flipped on the television – a variety show from Veritas called *The Tits and Ass Hour*. 'In your private opinion.'

'It's ugly, in fact. Wrong and ugly.'

'What is? Christmas?'

'Lying to Toby. He wants to know the truth.'

'What truth?'

'He's going to die soon.'

'He's not going to die soon.' I realized Martina meant well, but I still felt betrayed. 'Whose side are you on, anyway?'

'Toby's.'

I shuddered. 'Indeed. Well even if he *is* really, really sick, he certainly shouldn't hear about it.'

'He's dying, Jack. He's dying, and he wants someone to be honest with him.'

On the TV screen, a toothy woman removed the bikini top of her bathing suit, faced the camera and said, 'Here it is, guys! This is why you all tuned in!'

I shut off the set. The image imploded to a point of light and vanished. 'All this negativism, Martina – you sound like my wife.'

'Don't be a coward.'

'Coward? *Coward?* No coward would put up with the shit I've been through.' I chopped at the nearest plant with the edge of my hand, breaking off a glass frond. 'Besides, he doesn't even know what death is. He wouldn't understand.'

'He would.'

'Let's get something straight. Toby's going to have the greatest Christmas a boy could possibly imagine. Do you understand? The absolute greatest, bar none.'

'Fine, Jack. And then . . .'

And then . . .

The truth hit me like something cold, quick, and heavy – a tidal wave or a falling sack of nails. My knees buckled. I dropped to the floor and pounded my fists into the severed frond, shattering it. 'This can't be happening,' I moaned. I shook like a child being brainburned. 'It can't be, it can't be . . .'

'It is.'

'I love him so much.'

'I know.'

'Help me,' I cried as I worked the bits of glass into my palms.

'Help Toby,' said Martina, bending down and enfolding me with her deep, genuine, useless sympathy.

7

On the last day of August, at the height of a seething and intractable heat wave, Christmas came to the Centre for Creative Wellness. Sleigh bells jangled crisply in the hallway; the triumphant strains of 'Hark, the Herald Angels Sing' flowed forth from a portable CD player; the keen verdant odour of evergreen boughs filled the air. I'll never forget the smile that beamed from Toby's dry, cyan face when his friend Saint Nicholas waddled into the room dragging a huge sack, a canvas mass of tantalizing bulges and auspicious bumps.

'Hi, Santa.'

'Look, Toby, these are for you!' Sebastian Arboria opened the sack, and the whole glorious lot flowed out, everything I'd told Anthony Raines to bring down from the City of Truth: the plush giraffe and the android clown, the snare drum and the ice skates, the backgammon set and the Steve Carlton baseball glove.

'Wow! Oh, wow!' Bravely, wincingly, Toby tore off his oxygen mask. 'For *me* – they're all for *me*?'

'All for you,' said Sebastian.

Toby held his stuffed baboon over the edge of the bed. 'Look, Barnaby. Look what we got.'

An entourage of HEART members appeared, a score of pixies, fairies, elves and gnomes festooned with holly wreaths and mistletoe sprigs, streaming toward Toby's bed. One of Santa's helpers arrived pushing a hospital gurney on which sat a Happy Land even more elaborate than the layout my niece received after her burn (Toby's included a funhouse and a parachute jump, plus a steam-powered passenger train running around the perimeter). Three other helpers bore an enormous tree – a bushy Scotch pine hung with glassy ornaments, sparkling tinsel and dormant electric lights, shedding its needles everywhere.

'Hi, everybody – I'm Toby,' he mumbled as the helpers

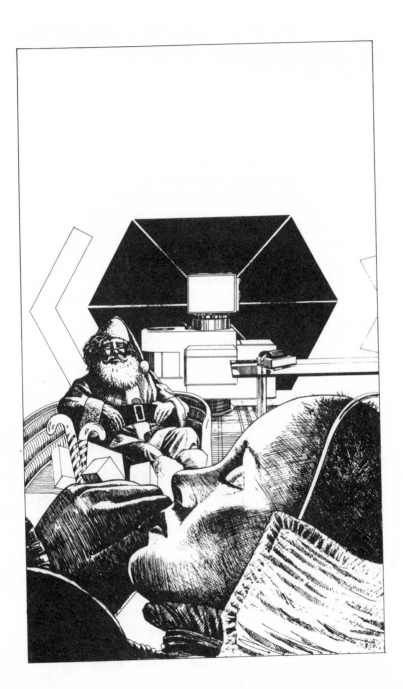

patted his naked head. 'I've got Xavier's Plague, but I won't die. Children don't die, Dr Krakower said.'

'Of *course* you won't die,' said the elf behind the gurney.

A tall pixie in a feather cap, holly necklace and lederhosen marched toward me. 'Anthony Raines,' he said. I had anticipated his physiognomy in every particular but one; far from sporting a moustache, his lip was as hairless as a sentient Satirevian stone. 'It's a privilege to meet someone of your spiritual intensity, Jack.'

A gnome connected plug to socket, and the Christmas tree ignited – a joyous burst, a festive explosion, a spray of fireworks frozen against a green sky. As Toby clapped his hands – an effort that left him breathless and doubled over with pain – the HEART members began carolling.

> Oh, Toby, we're so sad
> To hear you're feeling bad,
> But we can tell
> You'll soon be well,
> 'Cause you're a spunky lad . . .

'Santa, I have a question,' said Toby.

'Yes?'

'Did you remember that, er . . . that Power Pony?'

'Power Pony, what Power Pony?' said Sebastian with fabricated distress. He smacked his mittens together. 'Oh, yes – the *Power Pony*.'

Hearing her cue, a slender female elf rode into the room on a magnificent chestnut-hued Power Pony, its bridle studded with rubies, its saddle inlaid with hand-tooled cacti, a mane of genuine horse-hair spilling down its neck.

'What's his name?' Toby asked.

Sebastian, God bless him, was prepared. 'Down on Santa's Power Pony Ranch, we called him Chocolate.'

'That's a weird name,' said Toby as the machine loped over and nuzzled his cheek. 'Look, Dad, I got a brown Power Pony called Chocolate.' He coughed and added, 'I wanted a black one.'

A sharp ache zagged through my belly. 'Huh? Black?'

'Black.'

'You said brown,' I rasped. These final weeks – days, hours – must be perfect. 'You definitely said *brown*.'

'I changed my mind.'

'Brown's a great colour, Toby. It's a *great* colour.'

Toby combed the pony's mane with his pencil-thin fingers. 'I don't think I'll ride him just yet.'

'Sure, buddy.'

'I think I'll ride him later. I'm tired right now.'

'You'll feel better in the morning.'

Toby slipped his mask back on. 'Could I see how that Happy Land works?'

As Dr Krakower operated the mattress crank, raising Toby's head and chest and giving him an unobstructed, God's-eye view of Happy Land, Sebastian twisted the dials on the control panel. The toy lurched to life, the whole swirling, spinning, eternally upbeat world.

'Faster,' Toby muttered as the carousel, ferris wheel and roller coaster sent their invisible passengers on dizzying treks. 'Make them go faster!'

'Here, *you* do it.' Sebastian handed my son the control panel.

'Faster . . .' Toby increased the amperage. 'Faster, faster . . .' I sensed a trace of innocuous pre-adolescent sadism in his voice. 'Step right up, folks,' he said. 'Ride the merry-go-round, ride our amazing colossal roller coaster.' In his mind, I knew, the ferris wheel customers were now puking their guts out; the roller coaster was hurtling its patrons into space; the carousel horses had thrown off their riders and were trampling them underfoot. 'Step right up.'

It was then that I observed an odd phenomenon among Santa and his helpers. Their eyes were leaking. Tears. Yes, *tears* – children's tears.

'What's the matter with everyone?' I asked Martina.

'What do you mean?'

'Their eyes.'

'Step right up,' said Toby.

Martina regarded me as she might a singularly mute and unintelligent dog. 'They're crying.'

'I've never seen it before.' I pressed my desiccated tear ducts. 'Not in grown-ups.'

'Ride the parachute jump,' said Toby.

'In Satirev,' said Martina, 'grown-ups cry all the time.'

Indeed. I surveyed the gathered grown-ups, their dripping eyes, their wistful smiles, their self-serving grimaces of concern. I surveyed them – and understood them. Yes, no question, they were enjoying this grotesque soap opera. They were loving every minute of it.

Toby was no longer saying, 'Step right up.' He was no longer saying anything. The only sound coming from him was a low, soft moan, like wind whistling down the Jordan River.

A flurry of grim, efficient movement: Krakower cranking Toby's mattress to a horizontal position, turning on his inhalator, opening the meperidine stopcock. Anthony Raines took my son's knobby hand and gave it a reassuring squeeze.

'Will I see you people again?' asked Toby as the drug soaked into his brain. 'Will you come *next* Christmas?'

'Of course.'

'Promise?'

'We'll be back, Toby. You bet.'

'I don't think there'll be a next Christmas,' my son said.

'You mustn't believe that,' said Anthony.

I lurched away, staring at the tree ornaments. A Styrofoam snowman held a placard saying, GET WELL, TOBY. A ceramic angel waved a banner declaring, WE'RE WITH YOU, SON. A plastic icicle skewered an index card reading, WITH PAIN COMES WISDOM.

Turning, I tracked a large, silvery tear as it rolled down Santa Claus's cheek. 'Of *course* there'll be a next Christmas,' I said mechanically.

Toby's blue skin, stretched tight over cheek and jawbone, crinkled when he yawned. 'I love Christmas,' he said. 'I really love it. Will I die today, Santa? I'm so cold.'

Sebastian said, 'That's no way to talk, Toby.'

'You're crying, Santa. You're . . .'

'I'm not crying,' said Sebastian, wiping his tears with his mittens.

'Thank you so much, Santa,' Toby mumbled, adrift in

92

meperidine. 'This was the greatest day of my whole life. I love you, Santa. I wish my Power Pony were black . . .'

My son slept, snoring and wheezing. I turned to Martina. Our gazes met, fused. 'Tell them to get out,' I said in a quavering voice. Martina frowned. 'These HEART vultures,' I elaborated. 'I want them out. Now.'

'I don't think you get it, Jack. They're here for the long haul. They came to—'

'I *know* why they came.' They'd come to see my child suffocate; they'd come to revel in the maudlin splendour of it all. 'Tell them to leave,' I said. 'Tell them.'

Martina moved among Santa's helpers, explaining that I needed some private time with Toby. They responded like wronged, indignant ten-year-olds: pouty lips, clenched teeth, tight fists. They stomped their feet on the bright yellow floor.

Slowly the HEART filed out, offering me their ersatz support, sprinkling their condolences with Satirevian remarks. 'It's a journey, Mr Sperry, not an ending.' 'He's entering the next phase of the great cycle.' 'Reincarnation, we now know, occurs at the exact moment of passing.'

As Anthony Raines reached the door, I brushed his holly necklace and said, 'Thanks for hunting down those toys.'

'We think you're being selfish,' he replied snappishly, twisting the feather in his cap. 'We've done so much for you, and now you're going to—'

'Cheat you out of his death? Yes, that's perfectly true. I'm going to cheat you.'

'I thought you wanted us to synch your son's immune system with the cosmic pulse. I thought we were supposed to—'

'I don't believe that business any more,' I confessed. 'I probably never did. I was lying to myself.'

'Let's leave him alone.' Sebastian pressed his amplified belly against Anthony. 'I don't think he needs us right now.'

'Some people are so fickle,' said Anthony, following Santa Claus out of the room. 'Some people . . .'

At last I was alone, standing amid the grotesquely merry clutter, my ears vibrating with the ominous tom-tom of Toby's inhalator. Christmas tree, Power Pony, Happy Land, plush giraffe, android clown, snare drum, ice skates, backgammon set, Steve Carlton baseball glove – foolish, worthless, impotent; but now, finally, I would give him what he wanted.

Toby awoke at midnight, coughing and shivering, gripped by a 105-degree fever.

The August air was moist, heavy, coagulated; it felt like warm glue. Rising from the cot, I hugged my son, rapped my knuckles on his rocket jockey's oxygen supply, and said, 'Buddy, I have something to tell you. Something bad.'

'Huh?' Toby tightened his grip on Barnaby Baboon.

I chewed my inner cheeks. 'About this Xavier's Plague. The thing is, it's a very, very bad disease. Very bad.' Pain razored through my tongue as I bit down. 'You're not going to get well, Toby. You're simply not.'

'I don't understand.' His eyes lay deep in their bony canyons; the brows and lashes had grown sparse, making his stare even larger, sadder, more fearful. 'You said Mr Medicine would fix me.'

'I lied.'

'Lied? What do you mean?'

'I wanted you to be happy.'

'You *lied*? How could you even *do* that?'

'This Satirev – it's different from our old city, very different. If you stay down here long enough, you can learn to say *anything*.'

Anger rushed to his face, red blood pounding against blue skin. 'But – but Santa Claus brought me a *Power Pony*!'

'I know. I'm sorry, Toby. I'm so terribly, terribly sorry.'

'I want to ride my Power Pony!' He wept – wept like the betrayed seven-year-old he was. His tears hit his mask, flowing along the smooth plastic curves. 'I want to ride Chocolate!'

'You can't ride him, Toby. I'm so sorry.'

'I knew it!' he screamed. 'I just *knew* it!'

'How did you know?'

'I *knew* it!'

A protracted, intolerable minute passed, broken by the

interlaced poundings of the inhalator and Toby's sobs. He kissed his baboon. He asked, 'When?'

'Soon.' A hard, gristly knot formed in my windpipe. 'Maybe this week.'

'You *lied* to me. I hate you. I didn't want Santa to get me a *brown* Power Pony, I wanted a *black* one. I hate you!'

'Don't be mean to me, Toby.'

'Chocolate is a *stupid* name for a Power Pony.'

'Please, Toby . . .'

'I hate you.'

'Why are you being mean to me? Please don't be mean.'

Another wordless minute, marked by the relentless throb of the inhalator. 'I can't tell you why,' he said at last.

'Tell me.'

He pulled off his mask. 'No.'

Absently I unhooked a plaster Wise Man from my son's Christmas tree. 'I'm so stupid,' I said.

'You're not stupid, Dad.' Mucus dribbled from Toby's nose. 'What happens after somebody dies?'

'I don't know.'

'What do you *think* happens?'

'Well, I suppose everything stops. It just . . . stops.'

Toby ran a finger along the sleek rubbery curve of his meperidine tube. 'Dad, there's something I never told you. You know my baboon here, Barnaby? He's got Xavier's Plague too.'

'Oh? That's sad.'

'As a matter of fact, he's *dead* from it. He's completely dead. Barnaby just . . . stopped.'

'I see.'

'He wants to be buried pretty soon. He's dead. He wants to be buried at sea.'

I crushed the Wise Man in my palm. 'At sea? Sure, Toby.'

'Like in that book we read. He wants to be buried like Corbeau the Pirate.'

'Of course.'

Toby patted the baboon's corpse. 'Can I see Mom before I die? Can I see her?'

'We'll go see Mom tomorrow.'

'Are you lying?'

'No.'

A smile formed on Toby's fissured lips. 'Can I play with Happy Land now?'

'Sure.' I closed my eyes so tightly I half expected to push them into my brain. 'Do you want to hold the control panel?'

'I don't feel strong enough. I'm so cold. I love you, Dad. I don't hate you. When I'm mean to you, it's for a *reason*.'

'What reason?'

'I don't want you to miss me too much.'

It would happen to me now, I knew: the tear business. Reaching under his bed, I worked the crank, gradually bringing Toby's vacant gaze within range of his amusement park. Such a self-referential reality, that toy – how like Veritas, I thought, how like Satirev. Anyone who inhabited such a circumscribed world, who actually took up residence, would certainly, in the long run, go mad.

'You won't miss me too much, will you?'

'I'll miss you, Toby. I'll miss you every single minute I'm alive.'

'Dad – you're crying.'

'You can play with Happy Land as long as you like,' I said, operating the dials on the control panel. 'I love you so much, Toby.' The carousel turned, the ferris wheel spun, the roller coaster dipped and looped. 'I love you so much.'

'Faster, Dad. Make them go faster.'

And I did.

We spent the morning after Christmas outfitting a litter with the necessities of Xavier's amelioration, turning it into a travelling Centre for the Palliative Treatment of Hopeless Diseases: tubing, aluminium stands, oxygen tank, inhalator. Dr Krakower placed a vial of morphine in our carton of IV bottles, just in case the pain became more than meperidine could handle. 'I'd be happy to come with you,' she said.

'The truth of the matter,' I replied, 'is that in a day or two Toby will be dead – am I right? He's beyond medical science.'

'You can't put a timetable on these things,' said Krakower.

'He'll be dead before the week's out. You might as well stay.'

Martina and I carried Toby through Satirev to the Third and Bruno storm tunnel, Ira Temple riding close behind on the Power Pony, then came William Bell, dragging my son's Christmas presents in Santa's canvas sack. Toby was so thin the blankets threatened to swallow him whole; his little head, lolling on the pillow, seemed disembodied, a side-show freak, a Grand Guignol prop. He clutched his stuffed baboon with a strange paternal desperation: Rumpelstiltskin finally gets his baby.

By noon Toby was with his stalwart, Veritasian mother, drooping over her arms like a matador's cape.

'Does he know how sick he is?' she asked me.

'I told him the truth,' I admitted.

'This will sound strange, Jack, but ... I wish he didn't know.' Helen gasped in astonishment as a drop of salt water popped from her eye, rolled down her cheek and hit the floor. 'I wish you'd lied to him.'

'On the whole, truth is best,' I asserted. 'That's a tear,' I noted.

'Of course it's a tear,' Helen replied testily.

'It means—'

'I *know* what it means.'

Weeping, we bore Toby to his room and set his marionette-like body on the mattress. 'Mom, did you see my Power Pony?' he gasped as William and Ira rigged up his meperidine drip. 'Isn't he super? His name's Chocolate.'

'It's quite a nice toy,' Helen said.

'I'm cold, Mom. I hurt all over.'

'This will help,' I said, opening the stopcock.

'I got a Happy Land, too. Santa brought it.'

Helen's face darkened with the same bewilderment she'd displayed on seeing her tear. 'Who?'

'Santa Claus. Saint Nicholas. The fat man who goes around the world giving children toys.'

'That doesn't happen, Toby. There is no Santa Claus.'

'There *is*. He visited me. Am I going to die, Mom?'

'Yes.'

'Forever?'

'Yes. Forever. I'd give almost anything to make you well, Toby. Anything.'

'I know, Mom. It's . . . all right. I'm . . . tired. So . . . sleepy.'

I sensed his mind leaking away, his soul flowing out of him. Don't die, Toby, I thought. Oh, please, please, *don't* . . .

'If you want,' said Martina, 'I'll watch over him awhile.'

'Yes,' I replied. 'Good.'

Stunned, drained, the rest of us wandered into the living room, a space now clogged with terrible particulars, the Power Pony, the plush giraffe, all of it. Helen offered to make some lunch – sliced Edible Cheddar on Respectable Rye – but no one was hungry. Collecting by the picture window, we looked down at the City of Truth. Veritas, the vera-city; curiously, the pun had never occurred to me before.

I followed William and Ira to the elevator, mumbling my incoherent gratitude. Unlike the HEART members, they sympathized tastefully; their melancholy was measured, their tears small and rationed. Only as the elevator door slammed shut did I hear William cry out, 'It isn't *fair*!'

Indeed.

I staggered into Toby's room. He shivered as he slept: cold dreams. Helen and Martina stood over him, my wife fidgeting with a glass of Scotch, my one-time lover rooted like a moneytree. 'Stay,' I told Martina. 'That's all right, isn't it, Helen? She's Toby's friend.'

Instead of answering, Helen simply stared at Martina and said, 'You're exactly as I imagined you'd be. I guess you can't help looking like a slut.'

'Helen, we're all very upset,' I said, 'but that sort of talk isn't necessary.'

My wife finished her Scotch and slumped onto the floor. 'I'm upset,' she agreed.

'Toby was so happy to see you,' Martina told her. 'I'll bet he'll start doing a lot better now that you're with him.'

'Don't lie to me, Miss Coventry. I'm sorry I was rude, but – don't lie.'

Martina was lying, and yet as evening drew near Toby

indeed seemed to rally. His fever dropped to 101. He began making demands of us – Helen must bring his Power Pony into the room, Martina must tell him the story of Rumpelstiltskin. I suspected that the infusion of familiarity – these precious glimpses of his wallpaper, closet door, postcard collection and benighted carpentry projects – was having a placebo effect.

Placebos were lies.

While Martina entertained Toby with a facetious retelling of Rumpelstiltskin, a version in which the miller's daughter had to spin bellybutton lint into peanut-butter sandwiches, Helen and I made coffee in the kitchen.

'Do you love her?' she asked.

'Martina? No.' I didn't. Not any more.

'How can I know if you're telling the truth?'

'You'll have to trust me.'

We agreed to keep the marriage going. We sensed we would need each other in the near future: the machinery of grief was new to us, our tears were still foreign and scary.

At five o'clock the next morning, Toby died. During his final hour, Helen and I positioned him on Chocolate and let him pretend to ride. We rocked him back and forth, telling him we loved him. He said it was a great Power Pony. He died in the saddle, like a cowboy. The final cause was asphyxiation, I suppose; his lungs belonged to *Pneumocystis carinii* and not to Veritas's soiled and damaged air. His penultimate word, coughed into the cavity of his mask, was 'cold'. His last word was 'Rumpelstiltskin'.

We set him back in bed and tucked Barnaby Baboon under his arm.

Guiding Martina into the hallway, I gave her a goodbye hug. No doubt our paths would cross again, I told her. Perhaps I'd see her at the upcoming Christmas assault on Circumspect Park.

'Your wife loved him,' Martina said, pushing the *Down* button.

'More than she knew.' *Bong*, the elevator arrived. 'I made him happy for a while, didn't I? For a few weeks, he was happy.'

Behind Martina, the door slid open. 'You made him happy,' she said, stepping out of my life.

I shuffled into the kitchen and telephoned my sister.

'I wish my nephew hadn't died,' she reported. 'Though I will say this – I'm counting my blessings right now: Connie, my good health, my job. Yes, sir, something like this, it really makes you count your blessings.'

'Meet us in an hour. Seven Lacklustre Lane. Descartes Borough.'

Helen and I sealed Toby's corpse in a large-size Tenuous Trash Bag – Barnaby Baboon was part of him now, fastened by rigor mortis – then eased him into Santa's sack. We hauled him onto the elevator, brought him down to street level and loaded him into the back of my Adequate. As we drove across town, political campaign ads leaped from the radio, including one for Doreen Hutter. 'While *one* of my teenage boys is undeniably a drug addict and a car thief,' she said, 'the *other* spends his after-school hours reading to the blind and . . .'

I pictured Martina writing those lines, scribbling them down in the margins of her doggerel.

Reaching the waterfront district, I pulled up beside the wharf where *Average Josephine* was moored. Boris sat on the foredeck, wrapping duck tape around the fractured handle of a clamming rake, chatting with Gloria and Connie. I fixed on my sister's eyes – dry, obscenely dry – shifted to my niece's – dry.

Thank the alleged God: Boris grasped the situation at once. So Toby wanted to be buried at sea? All right, no problem – the canvas sack would work fine: a few bricks, a few rocks . . .

He brought *Average Josephine* into the channel at full speed, dropping anchor near the north shore, below a sheer cliff pocked with tern rookeries. Wheeling across the water, the birds scolded us fiercely, defending their airy turf like angry, outsized bees.

Boris dragged Santa's sack to the stern and set it on the grubby, algae-coated deck. 'I hear you were quite a lad, little Toby,' he said, cinching the sack closed with a length of waterproof hemp. 'I'm sorry I never knew you.'

'Even though you can't hear me, I am at this moment moved to bid you goodbye,' said Gloria. 'I feel rather guilty about not paying more attention to you.'

'The fact of the matter is I'm bored,' said Connie. 'Not that I didn't *like* Toby. Indeed, I'm somewhat sorry we hardly ever played together.'

Boris lifted the Santa sack, balancing it on the transom with his hairy, weatherworn hand.

'I miss you, son,' I said. 'I miss you so much.'

'Quite bored,' said Connie.

Boris raised his palm, and the sack lurched toward the water like the aquatic armadillo Toby had caught and freed on the Jordan. As it hit the channel, Helen said, simply, 'I love you, Toby.' She said it over and over, long after the sack had sunk from view.

'It'll be dark in an hour,' Boris told me. 'How about we just keep on going?'

'Huh?'

'You know – keep on going. Get out of this crazy city.'

'Leave?'

'Think it over.'

I didn't need to.

I'm a liar now. I could easily fill these final passages with a disingenuous account of what befell us after we set Gloria and Connie back on shore and returned to the river: our breathless shoot-out with the Squad, our narrow escape up the inlet, our daring flight to the sea. But the simple fact is that no such melodrama occurred. Through some bright existential miracle we cruised free of Veritas that night without encountering a single police cutter, shore battery or floating mine.

We've been sailing the broad and stormy Caribbean for nearly three years now, visiting the same landfalls Columbus once touched – Trinidad, Tobago, Barbados – filling up on fruit and fresh water, course uncharted, future unmapped, destination unsettled. We have no wish to root ourselves. At the moment *Average Josephine* is home enough.

My syndrome, I'm told, is normal. The nightmares, the sudden rages, the out-of-context screams, the time I smashed the ship-to-shore radio – all these behaviours, I've heard, are to be expected.

You see, I want him back.

It's getting dark. I'm composing by candlelight, in our gloomy galley, my pen nib scuttling across the page like a cockroach scavenging a greasy fragment of tinfoil. My wife and the clamdigger come in. Boris asks me if I want coffee. I tell him no.

'Hi, Daddy.' Little Andrea sits on Helen's shoulders like a yoke.

'Hi, darling,' I say. 'Will you sing me a song?' I ask my daughter.

Before I destroyed the radio, a startling bit of news came through. I'm still trying to deal with it. Last October, some bright young research chemist at Voltaire University discovered a cure for Xavier's Plague.

Andrea climbs down. 'I'd be *deee-lighted* to sing you a song.' She's only two and a half, but she talks as well as any four-year-old.

Boris makes himself a cup of Donaldson's Drinkable Coffee.

Out of the blue, Helen asks, 'Did you copulate with that woman?'

'With what woman?'

'Martina Coventry. Did you?'

I can answer however I wish. 'Why are you asking *now?*'

'Because I want to *know* now. Did you ever . . . ?'

'Yes,' I say. 'Once. Are you upset?'

'I'm upset,' Helen says. 'But I'd be more upset if you'd lied.'

Andrea scrambles into my lap. Her face, I note with great pleasure, is a perfect conjunction of Helen's features and my own. ' "I hide my wings inside my soul",' she sings, lyrics by Martina Coventry, music by Andrea Sperry.

' "Their feathers soft and dry",' my daughter and I sing together. Her melody is part lament, part hymn.

Now Helen and Boris join in, as if my Satirevian training has somehow rubbed off on them. The lies cause them no apparent pain.

' "And when the world's not looking . . ." '

102

We're in perfect harmony, the four of us. I don't love the lies, I realize as we trill the final line – our cloying denial of gravity – but I don't hate them either.

' "We take them out and fly",' we all sing, and even though I'm wingless as a Veritasian pig, I feel as if I'm finally getting somewhere.